# A Flicker of Doubt

# Tim Myers

BERKLEY PRIME CRIME, NEW YORK

**THE BERKLEY PUBLISHING GROUP**
**Published by the Penguin Group**
**Penguin Group (USA) Inc.**
**375 Hudson Street, New York, New York 10014, USA**
Penguin Group (Canada), 90 Eglinton Avenue East, Suite 700, Toronto, Ontario M4P 2Y3, Canada
(a division of Pearson Penguin Canada Inc.)
Penguin Books Ltd., 80 Strand, London WC2R 0RL, England
Penguin Group Ireland, 25 St. Stephen's Green, Dublin 2, Ireland (a division of Penguin Books Ltd.)
Penguin Group (Australia), 250 Camberwell Road, Camberwell, Victoria 3124, Australia (a division of
Pearson Australia Group Pty. Ltd.)
Penguin Books India Pvt. Ltd., 11 Community Centre, Panchsheel Park, New Delhi—110 017, India
Penguin Group (NZ), Cnr. Airborne and Rosedale Roads, Albany, Auckland 1310, New Zealand
(a division of Pearson New Zealand Ltd.)
Penguin Books (South Africa) (Pty.) Ltd., 24 Sturdee Avenue, Rosebank, Johannesburg 2196, South Africa

Penguin Books Ltd., Registered Offices: 80 Strand, London WC2R 0RL, England

This is a work of fiction. Names, characters, places, and incidents either are the product of the author's
imagination or are used fictitiously, and any resemblance to actual persons, living or dead, business es-
tablishments, events, or locales is entirely coincidental. The publisher does not have any control over
and does not assume any responsibility for author or third-party websites or their content.

PUBLISHER'S NOTE: The recipes contained in this book are to be followed exactly as written. The
publisher is not responsible for your specific health or allergy needs that may require medical supervi-
sion. The publisher is not responsible for any adverse reactions to the recipes contained in this book.

A FLICKER OF DOUBT

A Berkley Prime Crime Book / published by arrangement with the author

PRINTING HISTORY
Berkley Prime Crime mass-market edition / June 2006

Copyright © 2006 by Tim Myers.
Cover art by Mary Ann Lasher. Cover design by George Long.
Interior text design by Kristin del Rosario

ISBN: 0-425-21056-1

BERKLEY ® PRIME CRIME
Berkley Prime Crime Books are published by The Berkley Publishing Group,
a division of Penguin Group (USA) Inc.,
375 Hudson Street, New York, New York 10014.
The name BERKLEY PRIME CRIME and the BERKLEY PRIME CRIME design are trademarks
belonging to Penguin Group (USA) Inc.

PRINTED IN THE UNITED STATES OF AMERICA

10  9  8  7  6  5  4  3  2  1

*To Emily,*

*for Scrabble, road trips, Mythbusters,*
*and white trucks everywhere!*

"Reputation is only a candle, of wavering and uncertain flame, and easily blown out, but it is the light by which the world looks for and finds merit."

—James Russell Lowell

# One

As my kayak brushed against the woman's body, I thought I'd hit another half-submerged log. The Gunpowder River was full of all kinds of debris, washed there from the banks in the heavy rains that had assaulted us over the past two weeks. Paddling through the water was more like an obstacle course than the smooth river I usually found on my excursions.

It wasn't until I looked closer that I realized what I'd brushed up against.

In a moment of panic I dropped my double-bladed paddle, but I managed to catch it again before it skittered off the sleek surface of the boat and into the water. Without it, I'd be hopelessly adrift.

"Harrison, what's wrong?"

I looked over on shore and saw Markum, a big bear of a man with wild black hair and the look of an ogre about him, standing near the concrete steps that led down to the water in front of the complex. It was funny how he had become one of my best friends in the world. To the casual eye, we had nothing in common; no mutual interests to forge the friendship we had found nonetheless. Markum based his business at River's Edge—my converted warehouse that featured retail shops downstairs and offices upstairs. My apartment was the only living space on the second floor, and it was perched above my candleshop, At Wick's End.

My name is Harrison Black, and my great aunt Belle had left me the entire place, including At Wick's End, along with a hefty mortgage and a caveat not to sell the place for five years, not that I had any intention of ever parting with it. The people of River's Edge had become family to me.

I could hardly bear to bring myself to look. "There's a body floating in the water," I shouted inanely. "She's dead. What should I do?"

Markum considered it for a moment, then said, "I could call the sheriff, but it's hard to tell how far the body will drift by the time he gets here. Do you have any rope with you?"

"Yes," I admitted reluctantly, understanding instantly what he had in mind. I was a candlemaker by trade, so the worst things I had to deal with in my business were wax burns and nasty customers; nothing in my life had prepared me for what I was facing. Markum was a self-proclaimed expert in salvage and recovery, though I'd never been able to pin him down much more than that on what he did from day to day. He didn't sound at all panicked by the situation, but then again, he was standing safely on shore while I was the one drifting six inches from the lifeless body.

"Harrison, you've got to bring her in," he said.

"I know that," I shouted a little harsher than I meant to. I wasn't sure if I was up to the task, but I didn't really have a choice. I couldn't exactly ask Markum to swim out there and get her himself.

I reached behind me and retrieved the rope I kept on board to tie the kayak up while I went exploring some of the Gunpowder River's coves. I was going to have to get a new tether after this. There was no way I'd ever be able to use it again once this was over. After I had the rope in my hand, I wondered how I was going to tie it to the body securely enough to pull her to shore.

Markum called out, "I hate to bring this up, but you're drifting away at a pretty good clip. You can stare at it all you want to, but it's not going to get any easier."

I hated it, but I knew he was right. Judging from the general area where I'd found her, if I waited much longer, I might not be able to pull her weight through the water back upstream. And if she got away from me and drifted swiftly down the river, I'd be haunted by the memory that I'd let it happen. Where could I attach the rope, though? Should I tie it to her hand? I shuddered at the thought. No way. How about her leg? That was too gruesome to even consider. There was a belt on her dress, maybe it would hold until I got her to shore. I hastily pulled my rope through it and tied it off. My hand had brushed against her waist by accident, and I nearly dropped the rope as the body bobbed gently from my touch. With a grim determination, I started paddling backward toward the steps of the complex.

I'd covered less than a dozen feet when my load suddenly got lighter. Blast it all. The belt had come off and I could see the woman drifting downstream again. I paddled back toward her, not daring to look at Markum.

For some reason I was furious with him, probably because he was safely on land and I was wrestling with this body.

I approached her again, then I saw to my horror that when the belt had come loose, it had somehow flipped her over in the water.

Staring down at a stranger would have been bad enough, but I knew this woman and knew her all too well.

It was Becka Lane, my ex-girlfriend. Her lustrous blonde hair was fanned out around her head in the water like a halo, and the peaceful expression on her face looked more like she was sleeping than dead. Her dress had bunched up near her waist when the belt had come loose, and I had to fight the urge to pull the errant material back down over her legs.

"Harrison," Markum yelled from the shore. "You have to get moving."

I ignored him.

Poor Becka. What had led her to this? I hadn't seen her in nearly a month, but I still felt as though she were a part of my life. We'd gone from dating to animosity to friendship, and I was going to miss not having her around. She had become a presence in my life, and her death was going to leave a hole that might never be filled. In my mind, I could suddenly hear the essence of her laughter and feel the soft tenderness in her touch as I stared down at her.

I did my best to choke back my emotions. I couldn't grieve yet. I had a job to do. Trying not to think about what I was doing, I tied the rope around Becka's chest. I nearly fell in as I pushed the rope under her shoulder blades, but I managed to steady myself at the last second.

It was miserable towing her back to the steps, but somehow I managed it. I didn't even realize I was crying until I tried to speak to Markum.

"It's Becka," I managed between sobs as I climbed out of the kayak and slumped onto the lowest exposed step just above the waterline. Becka's body was tugging insistently against my boat in the current, and I had to hold onto the kayak to keep everything from drifting downriver. I knew I should pull Becka in, but I didn't have the heart to touch her.

Markum patted my shoulder and said, "Harrison, I'm sorry." He hesitated, then added, "Millie came out while you were paddling in. She called the police, so they should be on their way." Millie Nelson, a plus-sized woman with brown hair and soft gray eyes, ran The Crocked Pot Café, a place where I took most of my meals.

True to the promise, I heard sirens in the distance. I started tugging on the rope to pull Becka out of the water when Markum said, "You'd better leave her there and let the police handle it."

I nodded numbly, and he started to stand when I grabbed his shoulder. "Don't go. Please."

Markum settled back down beside me on the step. "Don't worry, I'm not going anywhere."

Sheriff Morton, a tall man with a ruddy complexion and a mop of brown hair, came rushing down the steps toward us a minute later. "What happened?"

Markum said softly, "She was in the water. It's Becka Lane. Harrison used to date her, so take it easy on him."

Morton's face softened. "I know. Sorry, I didn't know who it was." Two of his men arrived just behind him, and they carefully pulled the body out of the water and onto the bottom step. What happened after that was lost to me. I felt the sheriff grab one arm and Markum the other as they pulled me to my feet. I didn't care if the kayak drifted away. The way I felt at the moment, I was never going out on the water again.

The sheriff shouted to one of his men to pull the kayak up onto the steps as Markum led me to Millie's place.

Morton released my arm and asked, "Are you all right?"

I managed to nod, but I couldn't bring myself to make eye contact. It must have satisfied him, though, because he left me to rejoin his deputies.

Millie stepped in as she wrapped an arm around my shoulder. "Come on, Harrison, let's get you upstairs."

Markum took a step back, deferring to her.

"Could I have some coffee first?" I asked. "I need something strong." The truth was that I didn't want to be alone, but the coffee would be welcome as well.

"Of course," she said, "Come into the café. I'll fix you right up."

I walked inside, nearly stumbling as I crossed the threshold. I was surprised by Millie's strength in righting me. She led me to a table near the back, and Markum joined me. Millie returned in a minute with three cups of coffee, and I felt the liquid burn as I gulped it down. We sat in silence, each of my friends giving me space, but staying close by in case I needed either one of them.

After a while, Markum looked outside toward the river and said, "It looks like they're finally finished out there. Are you ready to go upstairs now?"

"I'm feeling better," I said as I stared into the last dregs of my cup. As I pushed it away, I added, "I have to open the candleshop."

Markum said, "Harrison, you've just had a tremendous shock. Close the blasted place up for a day, or a week if you need to. Your customers will understand."

"And what do I do in the meantime? Should I hang around my apartment feeling bad about what happened to her?" I asked him. "Becka was my friend. Who am I trying to kid? She was a lot more than that to me, at least at one time. I'm sorry she's gone, but there's nothing I can do for her anymore." I was surprised to find myself crying again as I spoke.

Markum looked surprised by my outburst, but Millie just patted my shoulder with a comforting touch. "Why don't you at least let Eve handle things this morning? You can work after lunch if you feel up to it."

I shook my head, wiping at the tears that betrayed my words. "I can't. She's not coming in until this afternoon."

Millie wasn't about to let it go, though. "So we'll call her at home. You know she'll pitch in if you ask her to help you."

I started to protest when Millie added, "Please, will you do it for me? You need to take some time to accept this."

I was still struggling with the suggestion when the sheriff walked in and sat down heavily at our table, blowing out a bellow of air as he did.

Millie asked him, "Can I get you something?"

"I wouldn't say no to a cup of coffee. I've been up all night, and I'm starting to feel it."

She left to get his coffee, and Markum said to me,

"Harrison, if you need me, I'll be over there." He and the sheriff had a heavy dose of natural animosity between them, and they would never willingly be together anywhere, not even to support me.

After the sheriff and I were alone, Morton asked gently, "Are you up to talking about this?"

I nodded. "We might as well get it over with. I was kayaking this morning before I had to open the candleshop. It was a good day to be out; the rain had finally broken, and the sun was coming out. There was a lot of junk that had been washed into the water, though. At first I thought I'd hit a log, but then I saw it was a woman's body. I didn't realize it was Becka until she flipped over. I managed to tow her to shore. That's when Millie called you." I stared down into my empty coffee mug, then asked, "Do you have any idea what happened to her?"

He shook his head as he played with the sugar dispenser in front of him. "There were no obvious signs of trauma, so they're going to have to look harder. She hasn't been in the water long, maybe an hour or two at the most, from the look of her."

"So you don't have any idea at all what could have happened?" I asked.

Morton said, "That's right. I don't know, and I'm not about to start guessing. I'll let the coroner figure it out, and then we'll go from there." He paused, then asked gently, "When's the last time you saw her, Harrison?"

"Are you honestly looking for an alibi?" I asked, letting my words bite, not caring if he felt my hostility in them.

"Take it easy, I have to ask." When I saw the softness in his gaze, I knew he hadn't wanted to ask me that question, but I also realized that he didn't have any choice, either.

Fighting to keep my temper in check, I said, "We went out for pizza at A Slice of Heaven last month."

"So then you two were dating again?"

Millie brought him his coffee as I said, "No, we were just two friends going out together for a meal. There was nothing happening between us, at least not romantically. What about the guy who was stalking her a few months ago? Is he still in jail?"

Millie hesitated at the table and frowned at Morton—no doubt hovering nearby to offer me her support—when the sheriff said, "As of ten minutes ago he was. Listen, I'm not accusing you of anything, Harrison, I'm just trying to collect information. I know finding her like that had to be hard on you. How are you holding up?"

"I'm not afraid to admit that I've been better," I said. Millie must have been satisfied with the sheriff's softened tone, because she left us and went back to her register.

I told Sheriff Morton, "Everybody thinks I should hide in my apartment upstairs, but I want to get back to work. I need to keep busy."

He nodded. "If it matters to you what I think, I believe it's the best thing you could do. It will help take your mind off what happened."

He threw a dollar on the table and said, "Listen, I'll let you know as soon as I hear anything, okay?"

"I'd appreciate that," I said.

After the sheriff was gone, Markum came back to the table. "What did he want? Did I hear him right? Did he actually ask you for an alibi?"

"Don't start," I said. "He's just doing his job."

Markum held his palms up. "Sorry, I know I shouldn't push you right now. Listen, do you want to get out of Micah's Ridge? It's a beautiful day. We could drive up to Boone, cruise around on the Blue Ridge Parkway, and then have lunch."

"Thanks, I appreciate the offer, but I want to work. The truth is, I need to keep busy. It's the only thing that's going to help right now."

He nodded. "Say no more. Why don't I hang around though, just in case you change your mind? There's plenty of stuff I can do up in my office, and that way I'll be close by."

"Markum, I don't need a baby-sitter. I'll be okay."

He said, "Of course you will." As the big, burly man stood, he added, "Just in case, remember, I'll be upstairs in my office if you need me."

"Listen, I shouldn't have yelled at you before. It's just—"

He interrupted. "You don't have to apologize for anything. I'm just sorry you had to be the one to find her."

"Me, too," I said. "Hang on a second; I'll walk out with you."

Before I left, I walked behind the counter and hugged Millie, maybe a little harder than I needed to. "Thank you."

She smiled when I pulled away. "You're most welcome. If you need me, I'm right here."

"I know that, and I appreciate it, honestly I do."

Markum and I walked outside, and I saw that the kayak was still perched on the lowest step near the water.

He followed my gaze and said, "Don't worry, I'll take care of that for you."

"Don't bother. I can't see myself ever using it again."

He said, "You never know."

Pearly Gray, the handyman to all of River's Edge, joined us and said, "What happened? I was just getting out of my barber's chair when I heard there was some excitement out here."

I started to explain when Markum said, "Pearly, if you'll help me carry the kayak up, I'll fill you in." The kayak had handles on both ends for easy portage, but I normally just threw it over one shoulder. Markum was a lot stronger than I was, but I realized he was deflecting attention away from me by enlisting Pearly's aid, and I appreciated it.

Pearly nodded to Markum after catching the expression on my face. He had a full head of white hair that was nearly luminescent, and an IQ that was off the charts. Pearly had been a psychologist in an earlier life, but he'd come to River's Edge to work with his hands a few years before I'd inherited the place.

I said, "Thanks guys, I appreciate the help."

"It's our pleasure, Harrison," Pearly said.

I left them with the kayak and walked to At Wick's End. Maybe it was a good thing that Eve Pleasants—my lone employee and candlemaking mentor—wasn't scheduled to come in until noon. I was glad for the respite, and for the first time since I'd taken over the candleshop, I found myself hoping that no customers came in. It was a shock realizing that Becka was really dead, compounded astronomically by being the one who had found her body. Becka's sister had died a few months earlier in a car accident, and I had helped her get over her grief. Suzanne had been her last close relative, and now I had no one from her immediate family to share my own grief with. I needed some time to come to grips with what had happened, but I couldn't think of a better place to do that than inside my candleshop.

I was there twenty minutes when Eve joined me. Her normally dour expression had been replaced by one of genuine concern. "Harrison, I came as soon as I heard."

"You're not scheduled to work until noon," I said. "Let me guess. Millie called you."

"She was worried about you," Eve said.

"She shouldn't be," I said, "And neither should you. Go," I insisted.

"Harrison, I'm already here. What sense does it make for me to leave and just have to come back in three hours."

I shrugged. "Go shopping, go back to bed, I don't care. Eve, thanks for coming in, but I'm going to be okay."

She took it better than I had any right to expect. As she started putting her coat back on, she said, "You're sure about this?"

"Absolutely. Don't worry, I'll tell Millie that you tried."

She was shaking her head as she left, but I was glad she hadn't put up a fight. Eve still knew more about candle-making than I did, but I was starting to catch up, and after all, it was my name on the mortgage now, and she knew it.

I was waiting on my second customer of the day when the telephone rang.

It was Morton, and he had news for me about what had ended Becka Lane's life.

# Two

"WELL, she didn't drown," the sheriff said. "To be honest with you, I think it kind of surprised the coroner, finding her in the water like that."

"So what happened?" I asked.

"It was sleeping pills," he said gravely. "She must have taken a ton of them. I'm sorry, Harrison, but it looks like she killed herself."

"What? That can't be right. It doesn't make any sense."

Morton said, "Harrison, I just talked to the man myself. He put a rush on the job. I'm afraid there's no doubt about it."

"But she hated taking any kind of pill at all. I refuse to believe Becka would do anything like that. I'm not saying she would never try to kill herself, but there's no way on earth I could ever believe she'd do it with pills."

He paused, then said, "Harrison, it's been a while since the two of you went out. People change, you know?"

"Not like that, they don't," I said fiercely. "I remember when she broke her arm six months ago. She wouldn't even take a whole pill to help her sleep, and she was in some serious pain."

"I don't know what to tell you," he said. "People change. She must have had some problems you didn't know about." His voice softened as he added, "More folks end their own lives than anybody could imagine. Not every car accident is an accident, if you know what I mean. I've seen more than one crime scene on the road that didn't leave skid marks from braking."

"So you're not going to pursue this?"

He snorted. "What is there to pursue? For whatever reason, Becka Lane decided she couldn't take it anymore, and so she decided to check out."

"And she just happened to fall into the river after overdosing, is that what you're saying?"

Morton said, "I admit that's odd, but the woman wasn't in her right mind. What are you expecting, rational behavior from someone who'd probably already decided to kill herself? She could have gone to the overlook to do it. A lot of folks go there. Who knows what she was thinking in her last few hours?"

"I don't believe it," I said flatly.

"Harrison Black, don't go stirring up trouble where there isn't any, do you understand me? I know you're upset, and I can imagine it's hard to believe that somebody you once cared about would kill herself, but you've got to accept the fact that it's over and there's nothing you can do about it now."

I hung up without even bothering to say good-bye. There was no way Becka would kill herself. She thought too highly of her divine right to exist. And even if she did want to end it all, there's no way she'd ever do it with pills. But it was clear that the sheriff was going to blindly accept the premise that she'd overdosed intentionally and killed herself. That didn't mean I had to, though.

I owed it to Becka to find out what had really happened.

I WAS STILL trying to figure out my next step when Greg Runion—Micah Ridge's gung ho land developer— walked into the candleshop.

"Harrison, I need to talk to you."

"This isn't a great time." Runion and I had crossed paths before, and I'd felt an immediate dislike for the man from the first time we'd met that had only grown stronger with time. I didn't have a problem with most real estate developers. After all, somebody had to build the places we all worked and lived in. But Runion had a slash-and-burn mentality, and I didn't like it in the least.

"I won't take up much of your time," he said, either missing my intonation or choosing to ignore it.

"What is it you want?" I asked.

"Since my latest downtown project was so successful, I'm putting a package together out here by the river. We could squeeze thirty condos and apartments into this building alone. I understand this place is tied up legally, but if you want to fight it, I'm willing to put my lawyers on the job. I'll make you a rich man, Harrison."

My great aunt Belle had given me the deed to River's Edge with the stipulation that I run the candleshop for five years, and though I knew I could probably break the codicil if I had to, I would have rather defaulted on the bank loan than go against her last wishes.

"I told you before, I'm not interested."

"You can't stand in the way of progress, Harrison. I'm coming out here, one way or another." He gestured out the window of my shop. "It would be a shame to lose all these trees around you, wouldn't it? Think about that."

"What are you talking about? Cyrus Walters and his sister aren't selling." Cyrus and Ruth owned a great deal of the land that abutted River's Edge, though they'd never done anything to develop it. Instead, Cyrus had cut a path for strolling in the undergrowth that ran along the river, one I walked nearly every day.

"You obviously haven't talked to them lately." The expression on his face made my stomach knot up. "If you change your mind, call me, but don't wait too long."

He breezed out of the shop and I felt my heart sicken. Was it possible that Cyrus was actually thinking about selling his land?

When the complex had been a warehouse factory in its first incarnation, Cyrus's father had bought up all of the surrounding land for expansion. When the factory failed, he was busy dying himself. The land went to Cyrus and his sister, and while Cyrus had stayed in Micah's Ridge his entire life, Ruth had moved to West Virginia to be closer to her grandchildren.

I walked out onto the walkway in front of River's Edge and looked at the trees that bracketed us. It would be horrible to lose them, especially to a massive block of apartments and condominiums. The construction noise and debris alone would make my life miserable, not even considering what would happen when all those people moved in right on top of me. The nearby location of so many new residents would probably help some of my tenants, but I wasn't sure how many of the Yuppies, Dinks and local social climbers would be interested in candlemaking.

I called Cyrus to see if Runion was just bluffing, but there was no answer at his home. In fact, his answering machine wasn't even connected. The phone rang for a solid four minutes before I finally gave up. I'd have to talk to him before Runion could persuade him and his sister to sell. I knew he hadn't yet, or Runion wouldn't have wasted his time with me.

Eve came back to the candleshop an hour before she was supposed to start work, but I didn't push it. I knew she meant well.

"Harrison, I can work this shift by myself if you want to go upstairs."

"I appreciate it, Eve. I think you all are right. What I really need to do is to get out of here for a while. Are you sure you don't mind watching the place by yourself?"

"Just be back before closing. I'd rather not take the deposit to the bank if I don't have to."

"I'll be back in plenty of time to handle that," I said. I walked upstairs, but skipped my apartment and headed to Markum's office. He was just locking up as I approached.

"Going somewhere?" I asked.

"I thought I'd grab some lunch. Did you shut the candleshop down after all?"

"No, Eve's handling things. Millie called her, and she came in early." I took a deep breath, then added, "I heard from Morton."

Markum's eyebrows shot up. "What did he have to say?"

"He told me what the coroner found. Becka didn't drown; she overdosed on sleeping pills."

Markum frowned. "Then how did she end up in the river?"

"The sheriff believes that she went to the overlook to think things through before she took the overdose, but it's wrong. Becka hated taking pills. There's no way she would have killed herself that way, even if she *was* despondent."

Markum asked softly, "And if she was, I'm willing to bet you're wondering why she didn't call you before she did anything, aren't you?"

"That's not the point. I'm telling you, Becka hated pills."

"So you're going to look into this yourself," Markum said.

"I've got to. What choice do I have?"

Gary Cragg, an attorney with his office close to Markum's, poked his head out his door. "Do you two mind? I'm trying to work."

"Sorry," I said, "We'll keep it down."

"Better yet, we'll take it outside," Markum said.

That seemed to mollify the attorney. As we walked down the hallway, I told Markum, "I thought you might like to help me do some digging, but I guess I was wrong."

He put a heavy hand on my shoulder. "Now what in the world gave you that impression? Let's go."

"But you don't agree with me."

Markum said, "You knew her better than I did. I

learned a long time ago to trust my gut, Harrison. If it feels wrong to you, the least we can do is look into it."

"What makes you trust my gut?"

He laughed. "You're all we've got right now."

We walked downstairs and I said, "Do you want to grab some lunch at Millie's before we go?"

He said, "Do you really want to subject yourself to Twenty Questions? I know she means well, but Millie won't let up until she finds out what we're up to."

"You're right. So where should we eat?"

As we walked to the back alley where my two trucks were parked—one bought and one inherited—he said, "If you trust me, I've got just the place."

"Let's go," I said.

As I drove us in Belle's Ford to Markum's restaurant choice, I told him about Runion's visit.

"One thing's for sure. He's not bluffing," Markum said. "I'd believe that guy was capable of doing anything. There's no doubt in mind that he'd sell his grandmother's burial plot if he could make a buck doing it."

"But what can we do about it? I tried calling Cyrus, but he didn't answer his telephone."

Markum said, "I don't know the man. Do you feel comfortable visiting him at his home?"

"Sure, I've been to his place a few times. He's pretty much a recluse, but he'll talk to me."

Markum nodded. "Okay then. First we eat, then we talk to your friend. After that, we start digging into Becka's life."

"It sounds like a plan to me."

Markum directed me to a place that was not much more than a shack on the outskirts of Micah's Ridge.

There were two dozen cars parked in front, pulled up on the grass, since there was no parking at all. There wasn't even a sign, though I saw a faded red T-shirt hanging from a nearby tree.

"Where are we?" I asked.

"Grover Blake, the smartest man I've ever met, lives here. He sells barbeque out of his backyard."

I got out of the truck reluctantly, following Markum's lead. "Is it legal?"

He laughed. "Harrison, look at these cars. This one belongs to the mayor," he said, pointing to a shiny new BMW. It was from the mayor's car lot. I knew he didn't make enough serving the town to afford to own it on his meager salary. "You think he's going to shut Grover down? Come on."

I followed him to a string of picnic tables and saw some of the most influential people in Micah's Ridge eating barbeque sandwiches and drinking Cokes out of glass bottles. Markum pointed to the lone empty table and said, "Take a seat. I'll be right back."

I tried not to stare at the people around me, but it fascinated me to know that this outdoor restaurant existed not eleven miles from my apartment and I'd never heard the slightest whisper about it. Markum came back with two big sandwiches wrapped in brown butcher paper in one hand and a pair of Cokes in the other, along with a thick stack of napkins.

I took the drink from him and said, "What if I don't like Coke?"

"Well, Grover's got a spigot at the side of the house."

"Coke's great," I said. The smell from the sandwich was amazing. "What's in this?"

"Just barbeque on a buttered bun. No pickles, no slaw, no sauce."

"It sounds kind of plain," I said.

Markum said, "Keep your voice down, Grover might hear you. Take a bite, then tell me what you think."

I took a bite, then another and another. Before I realized it, my entire sandwich was gone. Markum was grinning at me between bites. "It's good, isn't it?"

"Come on, it's better than good. How does he do it?"

"He swears it's because he recites Emily Dickenson to the pork as it's cooking. Who's to say he's wrong?"

I started to stand. "I've got to have another one. I'm buying this time."

Markum said, "Sit back down, Harrison. It's one per customer, no exceptions. Grover wants to make sure there's enough for everybody."

I found myself wishing I'd taken a little more time with my first sandwich, then I looked around and saw that several of the people eating were lingering over their food like they were participating in some kind of ritual. "When can I come back?"

"You can't, at least not without me." Markum finished his sandwich, then said, "Maybe there's something I can do about that, though. Wait right here."

I saw him approach a wizened old man the color of wet ashes. The two of them talked a few minutes, then Markum nodded toward me and waved. I joined them and noticed that somehow we'd managed to attract the attention of most folks there.

Markum said formally, "Harrison, this is Grover. Grover, this is my friend Harrison Black."

"It's an honor to meet you, sir," I said. "If I had a pen and paper, I'd ask you for your autograph."

Grover snorted at that. "Why would you want that for?"

"What I just had wasn't a sandwich, it was a work of art."

I thought for a moment I'd blown it, and so did Markum, if the tenseness in his expression was any indication. Grover stewed it over it for a full minute, then his scowl turned into a grin. "Nothing wrong with enjoying it, but I don't put on airs around here, Harrison. That's something you need to keep in mind next time."

"Yes, sir, I will."

Grover said, "And another thing. There aren't any sirs or ma'ams around here. I'm Grover, just that."

"Grover," I said, extending my hand, "it's a real pleasure to meet you."

He took it, and I felt the coarseness of his hand, brought on by manual labor, and years of it. "And you, Harrison." We all saw a woman approach, and Grover said, "'Scuse me a second, fellas."

A distinguished older woman I knew to be a judge over in Canawba County approached. "Oh, dear, I hope I'm not too late."

"Sadie, you know I'll always save one for you."

"Grover, you are a true Southern gentleman."

She put her money under a rock on the table in front of him, and Grover retrieved a Coke from the cooler beside him. After he handed the drink to her, he opened a homemade grill the size and shape of a fifty-five gallon drum. The full aroma of the cooked meat hit me. In a heartbeat he slapped melted butter on a bun, toasted it for a few seconds, then retrieved it and loaded it with barbeque.

She took it reverently, and Grover turned back to us. "Sadie's something. Now Harrison, I hope to see you next week."

"Do I have to wait a week?" I asked, unable to hide my disappointment.

"A week's not too awful long to wait," Grover said, then he slapped my shoulder. "Thanks for bringing him by, Markum; he brings a smile to my face."

"Happy to do it, Grover. See you next week."

After we were back in the truck, I said, "How long has this been going on?"

"For twenty years, the way I understand it."

I drove toward Cyrus's house and asked, "So how did you get invited for the first time?"

Markum smiled. "The same way you did. Somebody brought me. It's special invitation only, and you'd better be sure about who you're bringing, because if Grover doesn't like your guest, you're not welcome yourself anymore."

"Thanks for taking a chance on me. You said something that makes me curious. I know the man's a magician with barbeque, but why did you call him the wisest man you've ever known?"

Markum said, "Grover was one of the richest men in this part of North Carolina, but the stress of keeping his fortune growing was killing him. He had a scare from his doctor, a man Grover respected, who told him he'd be dead in six months if he kept at it. Grover told me he stayed up around the clock worrying about what to do, then he decided if he was going to die anyway, he was going to do what he'd always longed to, so he sold off his businesses, gave his money to charity and opened his barbeque stand. The doctor died seven years ago, but Grover swears he's never felt better in his life. Following your dreams is what it's all about, Harrison."

It was the longest speech I'd ever heard Markum make since I'd known him.

"I am," I said.

Markum smiled. "Why do you think I brought you with me? Now let's go see if we can find out what Cyrus Walters is up to."

I pulled up in front of the huge house, but it had changed somehow since I'd been there last. The place was starting to look ratty around the edges, with weeds growing in the front yard and one section of the porch rail gone.

"You'd better let me tackle him alone," I said. "He's a little uncomfortable around visitors."

Markum said, "I understand. Just yell if you need me."

"I'm sure it's not as bad as it looks," I said. Even though I'd been there before, I felt my pulse quicken as I approached the front door. What was I going to find inside?

# Three

I knew enough not to bother with the doorbell. It had broken long ago, and Cyrus wasn't a big fan of visitors anyway, so he had made a conscious decision not to have it repaired. I was expecting the door to be locked, but when I rapped loudly on it, it swung open, revealing a dark interior, though the day was quite sunny.

"Hello? Cyrus? Is anyone there?"

No reply. I glanced back at Markum, who was lost in something he was reading. No help there.

I stepped inside, a knot growing in the pit of my stomach with every step I took. I was in the grand foyer, a marble staircase in front of me and parlors to the left and right. "Cyrus?"

"Go away," a voice called from the left.

"It's me, Harrison Black."

"Harrison? What are you doing here?" There was still no sign of the man.

"Can I come in?" I asked, a ridiculous question since I was already standing inside his home.

"Stay right where you are. I can hear you from there," he said.

"Come on, Cyrus, this will just take a second. We need to talk."

There was a long pause, then Cyrus said, "If you can't abide by my wishes, then I'm going to have to ask you to leave. I mean it, Harrison."

I worried about the eccentric old man, but I couldn't afford to be thrown out before I had the chance to ask him my questions. "This is fine," I said. "Can I ask you something, Cyrus?"

"You may, if you stay in the entry," he said.

"I had a strange visit from a developer named Runion. Have you been talking to him about selling your land near River's Edge?"

"I'm sorry, but you're going to have to go." His voice was flat and tired, and the dismissal in his tone was readily apparent.

I couldn't just give up without a fight, though. "Cyrus, I need to talk to you."

"No," he said, more emphatically this time.

I hated being someplace where I wasn't welcome, but I had no choice. "Can I at least come back later?"

There was no answer, so I added, "I'm going to take that as a yes. Cyrus, can I bring you anything? I'm worried about you, my friend."

There was still no response, so I finally left. As I stood on the stoop outside the door, I wondered if I should lock the place up behind me. But then I realized that Cyrus had most likely left it unlocked himself, no doubt hoping for someone more welcome than I was. I ended up settling for pulling the door shut again as I left.

Markum looked up as I walked to the truck. "Did you have any luck?" he asked.

"No, he won't talk to me." I brought him up-to-date on what had happened inside. Markum thought about it a moment, then said, "And you say he's never acted this way toward you before?"

"I don't understand it. It's not like we were best friends, but this is ridiculous. We've had a hundred conversations, and it's always been face-to-face."

Markum said, "I'm afraid it can't mean anything good for you, then."

"Why do you say that?"

Markum scratched his broad chin. "Well, if he is thinking about selling out to Runion, he's bound to realize how it will affect you. That's probably why he doesn't want to face you. Most likely he doesn't have the nerve to tell you directly."

I started the truck, then said, "I hope you're wrong."

"So do I," Markum said. "Are you ready for our next move?"

"What did you have in mind?"

He smiled and said, "I'm in the mood for a little breaking and entering; how about you?"

"That depends. What did you have in mind?"

He ran a hand through his unruly hair. "We need to get into Becka's place and root around some if we're going to dig into her life. I'm sorry, Harrison, but there's no other way to do it. I've got to believe that if there's something to discover that made this happen, we'll find it in her apartment."

I'd never really thought about our next step, but he had a point. If we were going to figure out what had led up to her death, we were going to have to be bold.

I drove to Becka's new place, the one she'd chosen after leaving her old apartment because of a stalker. I'd been there once, picking her up for pizza. It was the last time I'd seen her alive, and I had to stop myself from taking that path in my mind.

On the way, Markum said, "I haven't popped a lock in years. I hope I still remember how."

"You may not need to. I've got a better idea."

He shrugged. "Unless you know where she hid the key, I doubt they're going to let us just waltz in there."

"We'll see," I said as I drove to her place. "If my idea doesn't work, we'll try yours." I pulled up in one of Becka's reserved slots and we walked over to her apartment.

Markum said, "I was kidding about the key. Don't tell me she left one under her mat."

"No, but she used to leave one outside at her last place. Becka was always losing her key, and she had a pretty cool place to keep a spare." There was an old fashioned knocker mounted on her door, one made of shiny brass, though the handle was slightly tarnished. "Great," I said, the second I saw it. "She had it installed here, too. It wasn't up the last time I was here."

"You're happy Becka put up a brass door-knocker?" he asked.

I reached underneath its edge, pressed a small hidden slide and part of the knocker's base popped open. Inside it was a key that I hoped was a match to her current lock and not the last.

Markum studied the mechanism, then said, "I've never seen one of these before."

"She used to date a locksmith, and he rigged it for her since she was always misplacing her keys. If you don't know the slide is there, you'd never find it. I'm just glad she had time to stock it with a key. Let's get inside before somebody comes out to check on us."

"If that's the right key," Markum said.

"I'm not even going to acknowledge that that's a possibility." I held my breath as I slid the key into place and was relieved when the door swung open. Markum and I slipped inside, then I returned the key to its hiding place and locked the door behind us from the inside.

Going through Becka's place was tougher than I imagined it would be. While she had always been perfectly attired, Becka's apartment was a continuing disaster area. Clothes were thrown all over the place, dirty dishes were still in the sink and there was a pile of mail spread across a tabletop near the door.

"Somebody got here before us," Markum said.

"No, this is the way Becka kept house."

Markum didn't say another word, but he did pull a pair of thin rubber gloves from his pocket. After he put his on, he tossed me another pair. "Don't worry, these are latex-free."

"Do you really think this is necessary?"

"Harrison, the last thing you want is for our friendly neighborhood sheriff to get interested in this case and start collecting fingerprints. You told him you hadn't seen her in a month, remember? Do you want to explain why your fresh prints are all over her apartment? Remind me to wipe off that key and door-knocker before we go."

I put the gloves on, hating how my hands began to sweat almost immediately. "Don't worry," he said, "You get used to it after a while."

"You've done this before, haven't you?"

He said, "Let's just say it's come up in the past. Now let's see if we can find out what she's been up to. Becka didn't keep a diary, did she? It might save us some time."

"If she did, I never knew about it."

Markum nodded as he moved to the mail and started riffling through it. "Okay, we'll do this the old-fashioned way. You take the bedroom and I'll look around out here. When we're finished, we'll trade off in case one of us misses something." It was a nice way for Markum to search the entire apartment without hurting my feelings, but I didn't mind. No doubt he had a great deal more experience doing this than I did.

As Markum started on the kitchen, pulling everything from the shelves and looking inside every box, can and container, I walked back to the bedroom. It was just as much a wreck as the rest of the place, but that didn't mean anything. I fought the urge to start cleaning up, then realized that if something was on the floor under the piles of clothes, books and magazines, I'd never find it. As I hung each dress and blouse back in the closet, I took the time to look through any pockets I could find. Going through her clothes, I remembered the large purse she always carried with her. Where was it, anyway? As I continued searching the bedroom, I kept looking for it, but I didn't have any luck. Once the clothes were hung up and the books and magazines were stacked in one corner, I had a better idea of what I was dealing with. The drawers of her dresser were just as unorganized as the rest of her place. I had no way of knowing whether anyone else had been there before us. There wasn't much of interest there, but I did find the torn corner of a photograph tucked inside the mirror frame, just enough left to hold it in place. It was of a clearing in some woods, filled with dead brown kudzu vines. There was a shape at one edge, maybe a barrel or a bucket covered in the dead vines, but I didn't have any idea what that might mean. I turned the photo over to see if there was anything written on back, but it was blank. Then I noticed a slight, hard to read imprint that had a date on it just four days old. I quickly glanced around the rest of the dresser space, but if the companion photographs from that roll were in the bedroom, they were hidden better than I could hope to find.

All in all, it was a rather unsuccessful search, so I went looking for Markum to see if he'd had any more luck than I'd had.

He saw me and said, "Good, I was just about to check on you."

"Did you find anything?" I asked.

"I'm not sure yet. Listen to this." He hit the replay button on her answering machine and I heard a man's angry voice. "Becka, I don't care what you say, it's not over. I can't live without you." There was a ragged pause, then he added, "You're not getting away from me that easily, I promise you."

"Who was that?" I asked, my skin cold from the sound of the voice.

"I'd say it was Becka's ex-boyfriend. Do you know who she dated after you?"

"Do you think I kept a log? Markum, I didn't even know she was going out with anybody."

"Take it easy, I was just asking. This character doesn't sound like he takes rejection well, does he?"

"How in the world are we going to find out who he is?"

Markum popped the tape out of the answering machine and said, "I know a guy who might be able to help us."

"Should we really be taking that?" I asked as I gestured to his pocket.

Markum sighed. "Harrison, the police don't care; the sheriff himself told you that."

"Yeah, you're right. I guess I just feel creepy being here digging through her things."

He said, "You can wait out in the truck if you want, I don't mind. Really."

"No, I'll stay."

He accepted that, then asked, "Did you find anything?"

I held out the edge of the photograph and he studied it a few moments.

I asked, "So what do you think it means?"

"I don't have a clue," he said as he stuffed it in his pocket along with the cassette. "Listen, are you ready to trade? I was about to check the living room, but you can have that if you want."

"Sure, that's fine." As Markum left me to retrace my steps, I looked through the small living room. There was a coffee table pulled next to one of the chairs. The table was covered with opened newspapers and a pair of scissors. I started looking through the papers until I found the only cut-out in the pile. An article about the size of an index card was cut from last week's paper. I folded the sheet and stuck it in my pocket, wondering what she'd thought was important enough to cut out. It meant a trip to the *Gunpowder Gazette*—a newspaper I detested—but I was willing to put my feelings aside if it meant finding out what had happened to Becka.

I finished up with the living room, straightening the place up as I searched. Markum poked his head out of the bedroom, holding up a folded sheet of paper. "You missed something," he said, smiling.

"I probably missed more than that. What is it?"

He handed me the note, and I saw someone had written in block letters: *STOP NOSING AROUND OR ELSE*. The words *OR ELSE* were underlined three times in a red marker, though the letters were all written in black. It made for a bold statement, no doubt about that.

"Where did you find that?" I asked.

"It was taped to the back of one of the drawers. I would have missed it myself if I hadn't pulled it all the way out. I found something else, too." He held up a fan made of money, all hundreds.

"How much is there?" I asked.

"It's an even grand. It was taped right beside the note."

"I don't get it," I said.

"Maybe she was blackmailing somebody and he got tired of paying her off. That might be all there is to this. What do you think? Was Becka capable of doing that?"

"I can't imagine it."

"Harrison, I know you cared for her. But take a second and consider it. Don't dismiss the possibility just because she was someone in your life."

I thought about how brash she always was, how single-minded Becka could be, and realized with some sadness that it could be true. "I guess it's possible," I admitted reluctantly. "So what do we do with the money?"

Markum studied the bills, then handed them to me. "You keep them. They might come in handy."

I refused the money. "Shouldn't it go to her heirs, whoever they are? The last thing in the world I came here to do was rob the dead."

Markum shook his head, and there was a sad smile on his face as he admitted, "Harrison, you're soft in ways that keep surprising me. Don't you think Becka would want to finance our investigation in searching for what really happened to her? If we use this right, it might buy us information when no other way can. I don't know about you, but my business isn't doing well enough at the moment to use my own money for bribes if we need them."

"No, I don't have a ton of spare cash just lying around," I admitted.

He offered me the money again. "Take it. If we don't need any of it, you can pass it on to her next of kin in good conscience; but truthfully, if her heir wasn't looking for this, there's no way it would 'accidentally' turn up. Chances are, whoever bought the furniture would be in for a surprise the first time they pulled the drawers out, and nobody would be served by that."

I stared at it the wad for a second, then took the money and jammed it into my pocket. The last thing I wanted was to be carrying Becka's money around with me. I couldn't imagine what I would do if Sheriff Morton showed up at the apartment, but it would surely look a lot worse with a thousand bucks stuffed into my pocket.

"Are we finished now?" I asked, worried more and

more about the money now in my possession than the fact that we were in the apartment illegally.

"I'm nowhere near it," Markum said. "Have you seen her personal files?"

"What are you talking about?"

"Think about it. She had to pay bills, keep track of things like that, didn't she? I don't see a computer around here. Did she have one?"

"No, I can guarantee you that. Becka was a Luddite when it came to computers. She believed the world was too dependent on technology."

He shrugged. "That's easy enough to say, but a lot harder to live by. So how did she keep track of her life?"

I scratched my nose, then said, "She had a personal organizer in her purse. Did you see that, by the way?"

"It hasn't been anywhere I've looked so far. Maybe it was near the point where she went into the water."

I shuddered at the thought. "The sheriff thinks she went in near the overlook. I guess we could look around there."

Markum put a hand on my shoulder. "That I won't put you through, my friend. After we leave here, I'll drop you off at the candleshop and I'll go look myself."

I didn't put up much of a fight, mainly because I couldn't stand the thought of going to the place where Becka had spent the last seconds of her life. I said, "I just remembered something. Becka kept her bills in one of those accordion files. It should be around here some- where. There's surely no reason she would have taken that with her." We both finished searching the living room and found the folder together. It was pushed into the corner of the room under a chair, almost as if she'd been working on her accounts the night before and hadn't returned it to its proper place.

Markum picked the file up and said, "There's too much here to go through right now. I guess we'll have to take this with us, too. Let's get going. We've got a lot more ground to cover before we can go."

I was about to reply when I saw Becka's front door handle start to turn.

# Four

"WHAT should we do?" I whispered fiercely to Markum.

"You locked the door behind us, didn't you?"

I thought back to the moment after I closed the door. "Yes, I'm positive."

"Then we're all right."

"Unless they have a key," I whispered, but at that moment I realized they would have already been inside if they'd had one.

I was about to breathe a sigh of relief when I heard a stranger's voice outside the door say, "I knew it was too easy. We should have paid off the super for the key first, just like I said."

More words were spoken that I couldn't make out, then the nearer voice said, "Give him a hundred, he won't argue. If he does, just take it from him." A pause, then he replied, "Because somebody's got to stay here and watch the door."

Markum grabbed my arm, held a finger to his lips, then he whispered, "We go out the back way."

He unlocked the sliding patio door and I followed him outside. At least we'd be out of the line of sight of whoever was trying to get in. I started around the side of the apartment away from Becka's door when Markum said, "Those aren't cops. I want to get a look at who's trying to get in."

I nodded reluctantly and followed him around the building the other way. A man in a nice suit was coming out of one of the apartments, and I wondered if it was our guy. After a minute, Markum followed him, with me close on his heels.

We were almost to the door when there was a police siren in the distance, coming closer by the second. I didn't know what to do, but Markum didn't hesitate. He raced for my truck, and I was half a step behind. I had the key in the ignition and was ready to start it when he said, "Don't."

"Are you crazy? They'll catch us."

"We want them to. You might want to take off your gloves before they get here, though."

I hadn't realized I was still wearing them. "Sorry," I said as I shoved them under the truck seat as he stashed the accordion folder under his.

"Markum, why are we hanging around here?"

"Our story is that we just got here ourselves," he explained. "Let those guys come up with a reason why they're inside. If Morton sees your truck flying out of this apartment complex, he's going to know what we've been up to."

"So tell me, what are we going to tell him when he asks why we're here?" I asked as the sheriff's car raced up.

"It's simple. We came to find the super to tell him about Becka so we could get the phone number for her next of kin, but the door to her apartment was already open when we got here."

I couldn't believe his audacity. "And you think there's a chance he'll actually buy that?"

Markum grinned. "Why shouldn't he? We just happened to be at the wrong place at the wrong time."

Morton got out of his car, glanced casually in our direction, then did a double take and approached us. "Don't tell me this is about you two snooping around where you don't belong."

I pointed to the open door. "We just got here. There must be somebody else inside."

Morton said, "Don't go anywhere," then pulled out his revolver and started for the door.

After two minutes, he came around the back way and walked over to us. "Surprise, surprise, nobody was there."

"They were there. We saw them go in."

The sheriff was doing his best to ignore Markum, a hard thing to do given the man's physical presence. "You. What did they look like?"

Markum said, "One of them was already inside, so we didn't see him, but we did hear his voice. The one still outside wore an expensive black suit. He was average, that's all I can give you."

"Come on, you can do better than that. Try."

Markum tilted his chin to one side, then finally said, "His hair was dark, but I didn't see his eyes. He stood a little under six feet tall and weighed about one-eighty-five."

"That's better," the sheriff snapped. "What else did you see?"

"Hey, all I got was a quick look. So who called you?"

The sheriff said, "A concerned neighbor called nine-one-one. Do you two really believe I'm buying your story?"

I stared at him as I said, "Frankly, it really doesn't matter to me what you believe. You still think Becka killed herself."

"Harrison, don't start with me."

I shrugged, but didn't say a word, though I'm certain he noticed the insolence in my expression.

Morton shook his head, then said, "What a waste of my time. Both of you stay here."

He took off on foot in the direction of the super's apartment, and after he was in deep conversation with the man who answered his knock, I asked, "What are we supposed to do now, just sit here and wait?"

"We don't have much choice," Markum said. "Give me a second. I'm trying to read the super's lips."

"Where did you learn to do that?" I asked.

"It comes in handy in my line of work." I saw him studying the man's face, and finally, Markum said, "He's not admitting to anything."

"Why am I not surprised?"

The super pointed to a nearby apartment, and Morton walked over there. An older woman in a bathrobe and curlers answered the door, and as Morton spoke to her, she looked squarely at us both. After a few moments, she shook her head and went back inside.

"Is that good or bad?"

Markum said, "I think we're in good shape, but don't say anything that might make the sheriff suspicious."

"You mean more than he already is?" I asked. I wasn't sure if there was anything short of a full confession that would make him surer that we were up to something.

Twenty seconds later, Morton was back. He said, "I'm pretty sure your mystery men bribed the super to get in, but he won't admit it, and without that, what can I do about it?"

"What did that woman have to say?" I asked. "And why was she looking right at us?"

Morton huffed out a breath. "I wanted to see if you two were the ones she saw going into Becka's apartment. She cleared you both. Funny, she gave me the same description you did, Markum. It was almost like she'd been coached."

Markum said softly, "Or it could have been that we were both telling the truth. Did you consider that possibility?"

"Briefly," the sheriff said.

I felt the weight of the money in my pocket. "So, can we go?"

Morton looked like he wanted to spit. "Go? You shouldn't have been here in the first place."

As I drove off, I felt the relief of our escape. "That was close."

"Not by a mile, Harrison."

"You're not the one with somebody else's grand in your front pocket."

"No, but that can be explained easier than the files under my seat and Becka's answering machine tape in my possession. Harrison, how would you like a drink?"

"A drink's the last thing I need in the world right now. Markum, what about those men we saw? What were they after? Should we just leave? What if they come back?"

"Morton's probably going to have somebody watching the place, and I doubt they'd invite us to their stakeout.

I don't know what those two were up to, but hopefully there will be something in what we found to point us in the right direction. Shall we meet up tonight in my office after everyone else is out of River's Edge? In the meantime, I can check around at the overlook, then paw through those papers and see what I can come up with."

"So what am I supposed to do?"

He laughed. "What you do best, my friend. Sell candles."

IT WAS A relief getting back to the candleshop and a world I was familiar with. Though I'd been forced through circumstances in the past to investigate a murder on my own, I'd never taken such an active role in things, and I was feeling shaky on new ground. I wondered yet again about my friend Markum and how little I knew about his life and his business. He'd been asking me for months to accompany him on one of his salvage and recovery jobs, but I wasn't at all sure it was something I wanted to do.

As I walked in the door of At Wick's End, Eve said, "I was beginning to wonder if you were ever coming back. Gary Cragg's been looking for you. He says it's urgent." She was in a snippy mood, and oddly enough, that just made me feel more welcome in my shop. I didn't want anyone tiptoeing around me. I'd had a shock, but there was nothing I could do about it except try to deal with it.

"With Cragg, it's always urgent. I'll talk to him later. I thought you might be able to use a hand," I said.

"Harrison, I almost forgot. You need to call Mrs. Jorgenson. I promised her you'd call the second you got back in. She's determined to talk to you as soon as possible."

"What did she want?" I asked. As my star candle-making student, Mrs. Jorgenson expected my full and immediate attention, and she paid for the privilege. There were times when the check from her private lessons made the difference between bankruptcy and solvency for my business, so I indulged her whenever I could.

"She didn't say. You know how she feels about dealing with anyone but the owner."

I had to laugh, since Eve still knew more about candlemaking than I did, although I was learning in great leaps and bounds. It was amazing how quickly I took to candlemaking, even with the motivation I had to learn.

I looked through the register receipts until Eve said impatiently, "Harrison, aren't you going to call her?"

I smiled at Eve and reached for the telephone. I had just hit the sixth number when the door opened and the lady herself walked in.

"I was just trying to call you," I said.

"I grew weary of waiting," she replied curtly.

"Sorry about that. I had quite a shock today. I'm not myself."

Mrs. J's eyes softened for a moment. "So I heard." Though the shop was relatively empty, she asked, "May we speak in private in the classroom?"

"Lead the way," I said, and followed her through the aisle to the backroom where Eve and I taught our lessons.

Once we were there, I asked, "So, are you ready for your next lesson? We're going to tackle pouring next, right?"

"That's what I wanted to speak with you about."

I felt a sudden icy ball in the pit of my stomach. Was she leaving my class—and my shop—at last? I'd been dreading the day, but I wasn't any more prepared for it than I had been the first time she'd walked through my door. "Go ahead. I'm listening."

She said, "Is there any chance you have time for a lesson now? I'm really quite eager to get started on pouring techniques, and I'm not at all certain I can stand to wait another minute."

Something must have shown on my face, because she added, "Harrison, I know you've had a difficult day. If you'd rather not, I understand completely. I do want you to know that I'm willing to pay extra for the privilege for such short notice if you're willing to teach me today."

"Mrs. Jorgenson, candlemaking is exactly what I need in my life right now. I won't even charge you extra for the privilege. Let me tell Eve, and then we'll get started."

Eve was watching behind me as I approached her and started gathering up some of the basic supplies I'd need for the lesson. "What did she say?"

"She's decided she wants a candlemaking lesson right now. We're going to do a pour if you can handle the front by yourself."

Eve nearly shoved me back to the classroom as I finished grabbing the last few items I needed from our stock. "Go. I've got this covered."

I walked back into the classroom and offered Mrs. Jorgenson the choice between using pellet wax and a solid block, and she didn't disappoint me.

"What's the difference between the two?" she asked.

I held up a bag of pearly white pellets. "These melt faster, and the results are the same as using wax you break up yourself. I thought you might want to save some time today."

"We'll break the wax up ourselves," she said firmly. "No shortcuts, particularly the first lesson, you know that, Harrison."

"Okay, here's the best way to do it." I chose a heavy block of translucent wax, then grabbed a flat screwdriver and a hammer. As I slipped on a pair of goggles from the selection on the shelf behind me, I said, "The object here is to break this block of wax up into small pieces so it melts faster. I like to have chunks about the size of a fifty-cent piece before I'm ready to melt." I put the wax in a large plastic container on the work table and gave it a few good whacks. Then I retrieved one of the pieces and handed it to her. "That's a good size." I started the water boiling on one of our hotplates and put the double broiler on. "The wax melts in here," I said as I added a few of the chunks I'd freed. "It needs to be around two hundred degrees before we're ready to pour."

Mrs. Jorgenson took one of the other pairs of goggles and picked up the tools as if she'd been using them all her life. She attacked that wax block like it owed her money. As I added her shavings and scraps of wax to the double boiler, she said, "I always thought each wax came to you tinted."

I showed her an array of die blocks I'd grabbed from one of our displays. "It's a lot easier this way. You can choose whatever color you like. You can even make your own shade or hue, if you're interested."

"One step at a time, Mr. Black. Let's make a basic

poured candle first: no dyes, no perfumes, no additives; just the wax and the wick."

"We can do that," I said, wondering why anyone would want to make such a simple candle, though not surprised that Mrs. Jorgenson had chosen that route. I showed her how to check the temperature of the wax with the candy thermometer—we weren't anywhere near where we needed to be yet—and then I showed her how to coat the mold with release. She'd chosen a small tin cone mold to start, one that came with its own base.

"And we just pour the wax straight into it?"

I shook my head. "The wick goes in first. Tie one end to this dowel stick. You can use a pencil if you don't have one of these handy. Now run the other end through the hole in the base of the mold." She tied the wick off, ran it through the tin mold, then I handed her a ball of mold seal.

"And this seal is for what purpose?" she asked.

"It keeps the wax from running out the bottom. Get it tight. Is your wick directly in the center of your mold?"

"I think so," she said as she handed it to me to check.

I glanced at it, then handed it back to her and said, "It looks good to me."

"What if it's not in the middle?" she asked.

"It'll be hard to change it after the wax is poured," I said with a grin, forgetting for a moment her lack of a sense of humor. I added quickly, "To get an even burn, you need the wick to be centered in the wax. Let's check that temperature again."

The thermometer read one hundred ninety degrees. "That's good enough."

"You said two hundred earlier," she protested.

"It's not an exact science, there has to be some feel involved."

She reached for the pot, but I stopped her and said, "First let's run some warm water over this jug before we add the wax to it."

"We don't pour directly into the mold?"

"I suppose you could, but it makes more sense to transfer the wax into something that's designed for pouring. The water warms the sides so the wax doesn't cool too quickly. Dry it off, that's good. Now be careful, that wax will burn you. Okay, that's enough."

She took the small jug now holding the wax and said, "Any other advice before I begin?"

"Pour it in slowly and try not to spill any. Fill it about ninety percent full." I watched over her shoulder, and when she'd poured enough in, I said, "That's good. Okay, stop."

"That's it?" she asked as she studied the results. "Why didn't we fill it completely to the top?"

"That will come later. Now we have two options. We can let it cool overnight, or we can rush the next step by giving it a water bath."

She frowned at the candle mold, then said, "You know I like to take things in their own time."

I didn't say a word, and in a few seconds she continued, "Oh, let's skip ahead. I must confess I'm eager to see how I've done."

I knew from some of our past conversations that Eve didn't believe in water baths. She was very conservative when it came to her candlemaking, but I'd been doing some reading and a little experimenting on my own, and I was ready to try it with Mrs. Jorgenson.

"Okay, get ready to put your mold in the sink. Don't

forget to use the oven mitts, it's hot. Let me add some water to the sink first." The water came just about to the level of the wax inside, with the rim of the mold keeping the candle itself dry. I added a weight on top to hold the mold down, then Mrs. Jorgenson said, "What do we do in the meantime?"

"Why don't we pour another candle? Would you like to make one with a few additions this time?"

She frowned, then nodded slightly. "I suppose some color would be nice. Let me see, a pleasant lavender scent would add quite a bit to it, too. Perhaps a shell or two as well?"

"That's the spirit. We've got baskets of things you can put in your candle. Choose whatever you like and I'll get started on another batch of wax."

By the time she finished pouring her second candle, her first attempt had probably cooled enough for the next step. I anchored her scented, colored, shelled candle in one of the other sinks after filling it to the needed depth, then looked at her first effort.

She asked, "Is it ready?"

"Not quite. Take this wicking needle and poke some holes all around the wick."

"Won't that make it ugly?" she asked.

"Remember, this is going to be the bottom of the candle. This lets the air pockets out. If we don't do this to your candle, it might not burn properly. Don't worry, we'll cover the holes completely in a second. I promise."

After she was finished with that task, I handed her the jug of original pristine wax I'd reheated and said, "Fill it all the way up now, but be sure to stop before you get to the top."

She did as she was told, and I explained, "Now we put the weight back on and give it more time to cool."

As she surveyed the candles in their respective baths, she said, "It's a little like making gel candles, but pouring is a great deal more involved than rolling or dipping candles, isn't it?"

"There are more steps, true, but there are also more variations." I'd read through half a dozen of our books and had seen some marvelous candle creations. It was amazing to me that anyone could make them, and I hoped to be good enough some day to try my hand at all of them myself.

She glanced at her watch and said, "We've been waiting some time now. Are they cool enough?"

"Let's check."

The first mold was indeed cool to the touch. "I think we're ready. Would you like to take it out, or should I?"

"I'll do it," she said, removing the weight and delicately pulling the mold out of the water.

"Okay. Take the mold seal off the wick on the bottom first, then flip the candle over. It should come right out in your hands." At least I hoped it would.

It slid out beautifully, landing in her hand with alacrity.

After cutting off the wick bottom—which was still wrapped tightly around the dowel—she held the candle up and studied it closely. "What caused this, Harrison? Did I do something wrong?"

I took the candle from her and saw a network of cracks in the face of the candle. They gave the piece a certain homemade look, but it was an appearance I was certain Mrs. Jorgenson wouldn't be pleased with.

"Let me check something," I said, pulling out one of

my reference books. I found the page on water baths and said, "I'm guessing the bath water must have been too cold. Sorry about that."

"It's my fault," she said. "I shouldn't have rushed the process." Then she studied the candle again and said, "To be honest with you, though, this presentation is growing on me."

"It does have a certain rustic charm, doesn't it?"

She said sternly, "Not that I have any desire to repeat the experiment."

"Of course not," I quickly agreed.

"Is the other candle ready?" she asked.

"Let's check on it." The cracks could have been disastrous, but it was pretty obvious Mrs. Jorgenson wanted her candlemaking to succeed. That was something in my favor, but I knew I didn't have too many more grace periods before she got fed up and moved on to another craft, blackballing At Wick's End along the way.

At least her second candle turned out beautifully. Or so I thought.

"This one has pinpricks all over it. Oh, dear," she said as I reached for another manual.

I found the culprit right away. "Okay, the wax was too hot that time."

"So much for the art of the pour," she said frostily.

I tried my best to grin. "Third time's a charm, they say. Shall we make another candle?"

"It will have to be another time," she said. "I'm nearly out of time."

"Let's at least finish off the bottoms," I said, desperate to salvage something out of the session. I heated a small metal disk on one of the hot plates and held the bases of both candles on it long enough to melt them into perfect flat surfaces.

She surveyed the results as I asked, "Shall we have our second lesson next week?"

"No, I'm afraid not," Mrs. Jorgenson said abruptly. Well, it looked as if I'd blown it after all. I just hoped we could survive her abandonment.

She shocked me by adding, "I don't think I can wait that long. Let's do it again tomorrow, shall we? I'm eager to get another crack at it." She arched an eyebrow, then added, "No shortcuts next time, Mr. Black. We do it by the book, the traditional way."

"By the book," I promised.

"Till tomorrow then." She picked up her new candles and started for the door.

"I'll see you tomorrow," I said, fighting to hide the relief from my voice.

So I hadn't lost her after all.

At least not yet.

# Five

EVE waited until Mrs. Jorgenson was gone, then said, "Tell me you didn't use a water bath on those candles."

I shrugged. "I would if I could, but you know how I hate lying to you."

The look of dread and uncertainty on her face said more than her question. "Did they turn out all right?"

I didn't want to admit my failures, but Eve would find out sooner or later. "Not so much. One was full of hairline cracks and the other had pinpricks all over it." She started to say something when I added, "Don't worry about it, it's not a problem. I used some of our reference books, so I know what I did wrong."

"Is she ever coming back?" Eve asked, her gaze at the door. She was as aware as I was that Mrs. J was extremely meticulous about her candlemaking.

"She wants another lesson tomorrow," I said.

Relief flooded her face. "No more baths, Harrison. Promise me."

I smiled. "Mrs. Jorgenson's words exactly." I glanced at the clock, realizing that it was nearly time to close. It was hard to believe all that had happened since I'd decided to go out in my kayak that morning.

Eve said, "Would you like me to take the deposit into town tonight? I don't mind, honestly."

I knew she hated carrying around the cash from our day's take. "No, I don't mind. You've done enough today."

She touched my arm lightly, rare physical contact from her. "Harrison, it will get better with each passing day. I promise you that."

"I hope you're right," I said. I'd managed to keep busy enough so that I hadn't dwelt on finding Becka's body, but I knew the night would be the worst, and it was something I wasn't looking forward to.

She said, "Should you see your doctor? I'm sure he'd be happy to prescribe some sleeping pills to help you through the night."

Eve didn't know that Becka had died from an overdose, so I couldn't blame her for suggesting it, but I still felt my stomach lurch when she mentioned pills. "Thanks, but I'll be fine," I said. We had four minutes left before closing, so I added, "Why don't you go on home? I've got this covered."

"I don't mind staying, truly I don't."

"I know that, but it might help me to keep busy. Good night, Eve."

"Good night then." I knew she was really worried about me when she didn't put up a fuss about leaving early. Normally Eve wanted to stay longer than I did, and I owned the place.

As I ran the reports from our cash register and started balancing the till, I suddenly realized that I still had Becka's thousand dollars in my pocket. What was I going to do with it? I surely didn't want to keep it on me all the time, but I didn't want it in my apartment, either. I went into the storeroom and pulled down one of the rubber molds from the back of the highest shelf. It was of a Christmas tree, and I loved the candles it made. I jammed the folded bills up into the peak, then put the mold back on the shelf where no one would stumble across it. One way or another, that cash would be long gone before people started buying Christmas molds again.

By the time I got back to the register the reports were all run. The totals matched the cash, so I made out my nightly deposit. As I was locking the door behind me on my way to the bank, I heard a car horn.

Erin Lane, the young woman who owned the canoe and kayak rental place on the Gunpowder River, was speeding into the empty parking lot.

I waited for her by the steps.

She said, "Harrison, I just heard about what happened. I'm so sorry."

"Thanks," I said, already tired of talking about it. If I didn't have to discuss my horrendous discovery every ten minutes, maybe I could convince myself it never happened.

As she approached me, she said, "I can't believe you found her in your kayak."

"Speaking of which, how would you like to buy one,

dirt cheap? I'm not going to be needing mine anymore."

"Harrison, you can't let this stop you from paddling. I know how much you love being out on the river."

I took a deep breath and tried to keep my voice calm. "Erin, if I never go out on the water again, it won't break my heart. Do you want it, or should I just put an ad in the paper?"

Now she was the one who looked like she wanted to cry. "If that's what you really want, we can work something out, but we don't have to talk about it right now. Would you like some company?"

I thought about it a second, then said, "Sorry, but I'm not in the mood to talk."

Erin nodded. "I understand that, and I promise; no questions. I won't say a word. I'll just keep you company."

"I appreciate the offer, but I'm tired and I'm not really in the mood for company. I just want to drop this off at the bank, then come back here and crash."

"I can take your deposit for you if you'd like, since it's on my way home. That way you won't have to deal with it tonight."

"I don't mind, really, but thanks for offering." A hurt expression crossed her face before she could bury it, and I wondered if she thought I didn't trust her. "Okay, I give in. Why don't you ride with me to the bank? I know it means you'll have to come back out here with me, but it might be nice having you go."

"That's great," she said, immediately brightening.

We walked back to my truck parked in its space behind the building and I held the door open for her.

"Thank you, sir," she said.

"You're welcome." We rode in companionable silence to the bank, and Erin was true to her word. I glanced over at her a few times, but she was looking out the window as darkness approached.

Finally, I said, "The streetlights are really pretty from River's Edge."

"You can see them from your apartment? I thought the trees would get in the way."

"I can see them," I said, not wanting to share the information that I had a whole other world on the roof of the complex. It was as private a place as I could ever have, accessed only through a scuttle in my apartment closet. My great aunt Belle must have enjoyed it as well, and I knew that sometimes it was the only thing in the world that kept me sane.

Erin didn't press me on it. I got out at the bank, made the deposit, then we headed back to River's Edge.

"Thank you," I said as we neared the complex. "You're as good as your word."

"I was glad to come along. It's not often I get to ride instead of drive. It always amazes me how much more I can see from the passenger side."

"That's not what I'm thanking you for, though I do appreciate your company. I meant about not quizzing me on what happened."

"Harrison, I'm your friend. If you want to talk, I'm here to listen, but I'm not going to press you about it."

I thought about it a second, then asked, "Would you like to see something really special? I'll show you if you swear you don't tell a soul about it."

"I'm intrigued," she said. "Where is it?"

I pointed to toward my place. "Upstairs in my apartment."

Erin laughed. "You certainly know how to get a girl's attention, but if you've got etchings up there to show me, I'm going to push you out of your own window."

"It's nothing like that. I promise."

"Then lead on," Erin said.

She followed me upstairs to my place, then I led her back to the bedroom. I noticed an uncertain expression on her face, but she didn't say a word. When I stepped into the closet, she was openly baffled by my behavior.

It was time to explain before she bolted on me. "This is the scuttle to the roof. It's where I go when I want to get away from the world. Nobody but you knows about it now."

"I'm honored," she said softly. I climbed the rungs, with Erin just behind me. I grabbed the flashlight from the hook near the hatch, then realized I had only one of everything on the roof. There'd been no need to have duplicates, since I was the only one who ever went up there. "You need to stay close to me," I said.

I flipped the hatch open and stepped through, then moved aside so Erin could climb up. She looked around in wonder and said, "Hey, you really can see the lights of town from here."

"Like I said, this is where I go to get away. I don't want anyone to know where I'm at when I disappear."

She nodded. "You have my word."

I led her to the storage bin where I kept my chair, blankets and umbrella. After pulling the chair out and setting it up, I offered it to her and sat on the bin itself.

She shivered in the chilled air and said, "Do you mind if I borrow one of those blankets?"

"Not at all," I said as I retrieved one and handed it to her. I'd positioned the chair so she could see the lights of Micah's Ridge, but not my face. It was somehow easier sitting there in the darkness not having to make eye contact as we spoke.

In the shadows, I began to talk. "I met Becka seven years ago. She was gorgeous, the kind of woman I ordinarily never would have approached, but she did that herself. I was at an art gallery opening in Charlotte where a friend of mine was showing his sculptures, and Becka was there with some friends as well. Her heel caught on the carpet and she literally fell into my arms. We dated off and on for a few years after that. It's hard to describe what attracted me to her." I paused, then said, "Okay, she was great-looking, but that only goes so far. There was something about her—a drive to follow her own heart—that attracted me. Was she perfect? Far from it, but there was a bond between us I still can't explain. Even when she was doing her best to drive me crazy, I still cared about her. Nothing romantic, mind you—not in the last ten or eleven months, anyway—but she was a part of my life, and now she's gone. . . ." I hadn't meant to make such a long-winded speech, and I felt embarrassed by it.

Erin took it all in, then said softly, "It's okay to miss her, Harrison."

I felt the tears come. I hadn't wept since Belle had died, but I couldn't stop them. Erin stood, moved near and put her arms around me, nestling my head to her chest. She stroked my hair and hummed softly as the emotion ran through me, until it finally faded. I pulled away and said, "Sorry about that, I don't know what happened."

"Do you feel better?" she asked.

"You know what? I do. Thanks."

Erin stepped away and said, "Thank you for sharing all of this with me, Harrison."

"I'm glad I did."

She looked up at the stars and said, "How could I not love it? Could I come back up another time?"

"That sounds great. We can have a picnic sometime."

Erin shivered. "Sometime warm, maybe."

"It is getting chilly, isn't it? Let's go downstairs. I'll make us some coffee."

I turned the flashlight on and led her back to the scuttle. "Do you have any hot chocolate?" she asked once we were back in my apartment.

"You'd better believe it. I've even got marshmallows," I said with a smile.

After we had our cocoa, Erin said, "This was fun. I enjoy hanging out with you, Harrison."

"Thanks, I needed this more than I realized." I walked her to her car, and she surprised me by giving me a peck on the cheek. "Call me any time, Harrison."

When I walked back upstairs, I found Markum leaning against my door. The accordion folder we'd retrieved from Becka's apartment was sitting on top of a box he had tucked under one arm.

I asked, "How long have you been here?"

"Not long enough to matter. I saw you had company so I waited until she was gone. Are you ready to do some more digging?"

The calm ease I'd felt with Erin drained quickly away, but I knew I owed it to Becka to find out what had really happened to her. "I'm ready."

We walked in the apartment and I picked up the

coffee mugs Erin and I had used for our cocoa. "Do you want anything?" I asked.

"No, I'm good. Listen, I'm sorry to do this to you. I know you've had the mother of all bad days, but our only chance here is to jump on this before the trail gets too cold."

"I agree," I said. "So what's in the box?"

He put the folder to one side and brought out a woman's handbag. I recognized it as Becka's. "Where did you find that?"

"It was in the water a thousand yards downstream from the overlook. I got soaked getting it, but it was worth it."

He opened it and pulled out an envelope. "Look at that."

It was addressed to Becka. Despite the water damage, I could read enough of the return address to see that it was from Washington, D.C., but the name of the agency had been torn off the corner. I opened the envelope, not sure what I was hoping to find, but it was empty. Then I flipped it over and saw a brief note scrawled in Becka's handwriting. The last few words were smudged and the first part was obscured by a smear of mud. All I could make out for sure was the single word "land." As a clue, it wasn't much use. If she'd used a pen I might still be able to read it, but the pencil lead had been blurred almost beyond recognition during its submersion. "Sorry, there's not enough here to do us much good."

I had a thought and said, "Wait a second, I'll be right back." I retrieved the photo fragment I'd found on her dresser mirror and handed it to him as I said, "Maybe they're connected in some way. Could she have been asking someone about this barrel? But how do we find out what they said?"

Markum studied the photo, then said, "The postmark on the envelope is two weeks before the date on the back of the picture."

I felt deflated. "So they're not related."

"Maybe, maybe not. Can I have this? I've got a guy who does me favors on occasion, and he might be able to give us something more than we're seeing here."

"Sure, be my guest." I took a deep breath, then let it out slowly. "This isn't going to be easy, is it?"

Markum said, "Patience, Harrison. We have to gather as many pieces of the puzzle as we can before we can figure out what really happened to her."

I leaned forward and snagged the purse. It had a mildewed smell to it, and I could feel some kind of slime on it. Becka was fastidious about her appearance—the state of her apartment notwithstanding—and I knew it would have infuriated her to see her purse like that. Instead of getting sadder, it only fueled my anger. Somebody was going to pay for what they'd done to her.

I started going through her purse with new determination. There was a grocery list there, her checkbook, half a dozen makeup items and an odd assortment of things that collect in the bottom of some women's purses. I found another telephone number—this one written in permanent ink on the back of a deposit slip—so I dialed it and was startled to hear Greg Runion answer.

I hung up the telephone, and Markum asked, "What was that all about?"

"I found a phone number in Becka's purse, so I dialed it. It was Runion."

"The developer? Why would Becka have his number in her purse?"

I scratched my head, then laid the paper aside. "I'm not sure, but it's something we need to look into." I studied the contents of her purse for a few more minutes, then asked, "So what's missing here?"

"I don't know, I was hoping you would."

"Her car keys aren't here. Did you see her car anywhere near the overlook? She didn't walk, that's for sure; it's too far from town."

Markum nodded. "You're right. There were no cars in the parking area when I went there to look around. Why don't you call your buddy the sheriff and see if he's looked for her car?"

At least it was something. "I'll give it a shot, but I don't know if he'll tell me anything."

"You've got a better chance of finding out than I do," Markum said.

I dialed the sheriff's office, and after going through the switchboard, I reached Morton himself. "This is Harrison Black. I need to ask you something."

"Harrison, I've got a hit-and-run that's driving me nuts. Some guy got mowed over by a car on the city limits boundary. Half of him is in Micah's Ridge and the other half is on county property. They're out there now trying to figure out where most of the man's body is lying. Make it quick."

"Where's Becka's car?" I asked.

"Come on, it was a suicide."

"She didn't walk from town, Sheriff. Becka wouldn't do that. So how did she get out there, and where's her vehicle?"

He said curtly, "I'm going to tell you, but only because

of the day you've had. We found her vehicle at the overlook. The keys were in it and the engine was still running. I know Micah's Ridge is a small town, but I'm still
surprised nobody stole it. Now will you drop this? She
killed herself."

I wanted to say something else when the telephone
connection ended.

"What did he say?" Markum asked.

"They found the car with the engine still running at
the overlook."

Markum frowned. "I'm sure that just reinforces his
belief that it was suicide."

"Not for me, it doesn't," I said. "Becka wouldn't
leave her car running like that. She used to give me
grief about running my truck in the winter to warm it
up. Over the last six months, she'd developed a real environmental conscience."

"And if he'd stayed on the line long enough for you
to tell him that, I'm sure the sheriff would have said that
she wasn't in her right frame of mind, or she never
would have killed herself in the first place. For every
new bit of information we find, there's a way he can
turn it around on us. I'm not all that surprised that we're
not going to be getting any help from him."

"So why do you believe me?" I asked.

It looked like he thought about it, then said, "Your
gut tells you it was murder. I'm going with that."

"Good enough," I said. "I'm not wrong about this."

"I never thought you were. Now what are we going to
do about it?"

I reached for the accordion folder and said, "We keep
digging."

# Six

AFTER an hour of searching through her personal papers, I was ready to call it a night. "There's nothing here that shouldn't be," I said.

Markum nodded. "I've got to agree with you about that. So what did we miss?"

"I don't follow you."

"Those two suits weren't at Becka's searching for decorating tips. Is there anything we found that they might have been looking for?"

"What about the message on the answering machine?" I asked. "Could they be working for the guy we heard?"

Markum nodded. "You could be right. So then who is our mystery man?"

"I don't even have a guess. Have you talked to your friend about the tape?"

"He's not going to be able to help after all," Markum said. "I'm going to get a Coke."

"I'll grab one for you, I'm thirsty myself. So what happened, is your friend out of town?"

Markum shrugged. "That's as good a euphemism as any. He's in jail."

"You know the most interesting people." I grabbed two Cokes and handed him one.

"You don't know the half of it. It looks like we're on our own with the tape. I should have taken her answering machine, too; I don't have anything that will play that size tape."

"I've got a handheld tape recorder around here somewhere. Don't they take the same size tapes as those old machines?"

Markum said, "I never thought of that. Get your tape player and I'll go get the tape."

After we met back in the living room, I held out my hand. "Let me try it."

"It won't work," he said as he handed me the tape.

I didn't even have to try it; he was clearly right about the tape's size. That wasn't our only problem, though. The tape was heavier than it should have been. I held it up to my nose and sniffed, then realized that it had gotten wet.

Markum looked disgusted. "I had it with me when I went after Becka's purse. It was a stupid mistake, Harrison. I'm sorry. I don't even know if it's still any good."

"Don't be so hard on yourself. It wasn't a mistake, it was an accident. There still might be something we can hear."

"So what do we do?"

"We go out and get a machine that will play it."

He took a deep breath, then said, "Do you really think there's hope for it?"

"The only way we'll know is if we try."

I saw Markum smile, so I quickly added, "I'm not breaking back into Becka's, even if we do have a key."

"Do you honestly think the Community Watch is working this late at night? If Morton even bothered with a stakeout, his deputies are probably long gone. Come on, we can be in and out in five minutes."

"Are you serious?"

"What did you have in mind, going to Hickory to Best Buy and listening to it on one of their machines? That's just a wee bit suspicious, wouldn't you say?"

"And breaking back into Becka's isn't?"

I grabbed my coat and he asked, "So where are you going?"

"If we're going to do this, let's get it over with before I change my mind."

"That's the spirit, Harrison. I'll make a salvage man out of you yet."

"Thanks, but no thanks. After this, I'm sticking to candlemaking."

Markum said, "I suspect that's the wisest thing you can do, but just think about the fun you're missing."

DRIVING THROUGH THE darkened streets of Micah's Ridge with just the lights from the dash illuminating us, I felt like a spy on a dangerous mission.

Markum must have sensed my mood. "There's nothing like it, is there?" he asked.

"Do you do this a lot?"

There was a pause, then he said, "Harrison, I get as much joy out of the hunt as I do actually achieving my objectives. How many people get to do something they love these days?"

"I do," I said. "I never knew what I was missing until Belle left me the candleshop."

"Don't you ever wish your life was a little more exciting?"

I turned into Becka's complex. "Honestly? Lately I've been getting more adventure than I care to."

"Park over there," he said, pointing to the general parking lot away from the housing units. I did as he said, then asked, "So we're actually trying to be stealthy this time?"

"It's an entirely different proposition breaking into someplace at night. I'd rather do it in broad daylight, but I'm afraid what we might find if we wait until morning. Follow my lead and try to make as little noise as possible."

I followed him around the gated pool, past the tennis courts and up to Becka's sliding patio door in back. He studied the interior through the glass while I kept watch all around us. There were a thousand noises in the night, and I had the creepy feeling that every one of them was after us. After what seemed like hours, Markum tapped my shoulder and motioned me to follow him.

We crept around the building and he hit the knocker's slide to retrieve the key. I'd only shown him once, but he had no problem finding it in the distant lights of the complex's parking area.

After a minute, he hissed, "It's not there. Are you sure you put it back?"

"You saw me," I said as I brushed past him. The key wasn't in its usual place, and I started panicking, thinking that someone was in the apartment. I almost said something to Markum when my fingertip brushed something in the bottom of the tray. I must not have put it back in its place properly, and I was lucky it had fallen inside instead of out onto the ground.

I handed the key to Markum, who looked surprised, but pleased. He slid it into the lock, opened the door, then replaced the key immediately. Once we were inside, the apartment was nearly pitch-black. I knew Becka always bought the heaviest drapes she could find, since she liked to sleep late whenever she could. A light suddenly sprang up, and I realized Markum had turned on his small flashlight.

"Let's just grab the machine and go."

"Easy, Harrison. We're here. Why don't we look around again?"

"Markum, we searched the place in the daylight. I don't want the sheriff to catch us in here."

"He's busy with a body on the county line, remember? Okay, I don't want to explain this to him any more than you do."

He unplugged the machine and wrapped the cord around it. "Are you ready?"

"Let's go."

We were back outside in less than a minute. As I stepped back to let Markum close the door, the porch light from next door came on. Without thinking or hesitating, I dove through the bushes and started running. Markum was beside me, then suddenly he passed me and was waiting for me when we got back to the truck.

I jammed the key into the ignition, started the truck and took off without looking back. "Man, that was too close," I said once we were on the highway again.

"It wouldn't feel right if I didn't have at least one adrenaline rush from all of this."

We got back to my apartment and quickly plugged

the machine in. I hit the play button after I put the tape in, but all we got was a garbled mess. Markum said, "So we took that risk for nothing."

"We had to know," I said. "I don't know about you, but I won't forget that voice anytime soon. If I hear it again, I'll know it."

"There was a lot more on that tape than the voice, though. There was something in the background, something I didn't quite catch that might have helped us."

I slapped Markum on the shoulder. "It's done, so there's no use worrying about it now. Let's call it a night. We can figure out what our next step is tomorrow."

He hesitated, as if he wanted to apologize again, then started to leave the apartment. "Tomorrow it is, Harrison."

"See you then," I said and ushered him out.

The tape had been a dead end, and Becka's purse hadn't been much better. All in all, it was a bad end to a horrible day, and the only thing I wanted was to put it all behind me. I found myself wishing Heather was out of town so I could have her cat Esmarelda for company, but I couldn't very well call her up and ask her if I could borrow her cat. Well, I could, and I knew she'd gladly do it, but I didn't want to face the teasing I'd get about it. For tonight I'd have to get through it without my feline friend. Talking to Erin, unloading on her, had done me a world of good, but my time with Markum had negated it. I considered calling her despite the teasing I would probably get, then glanced at the clock and saw that it was already past midnight. There was no way I could bring myself to make the call.

I wasn't looking forward to closing my eyes, afraid of what might haunt my dreams, but I stretched out on the couch to rest, and before I realized what was happening, I was fast asleep.

**BEFORE WE OPENED** the candleshop the next morning, I drove by the *Gunpowder Gazette* to get a copy of the newspaper I'd found clipped in Becka's apartment. I had my own subscription, but I'd already recycled mine. While I detested the owner and publisher of the paper, it was critical to my business that I keep up with the events of Micah's Ridge, and the only way to do that was to read the *Gazette*. Thankfully the newspaper office still had some for sale for that date, and as I was paying for my paper, Hank Klein, the *Gunpowder Gazette* publisher, came out of his office. "I thought I heard voices out here. How are you today, Mr. Black?"

"Fine. How's your wife?" I asked curtly. Wanda Klein had accused me of murdering my competition, and her husband had run with the idea until he'd found another suspect. There was no such thing as due process in Micah's Ridge, at least not when it came to the town newspaper.

"She's fine as well. Since you're here, would you mind if I asked you a few questions?"

"Taking a sudden interest in candlemaking, are you?"

He bit his upper lip. "Hardly. I'm more interested in how you found that woman's body in the river yesterday. She was an old flame of yours, wasn't she?"

"We hadn't dated for a while. We were good friends, though."

Klein said, "I understand she was quite promiscuous. Would you care to comment on that?"

I'm not a man of violence ordinarily, but there was something smug in the editor's tone, a look of prurient interest that made me want to kill him. I grabbed his shirt, startling us both, and said, "If you do one thing to smear Becka Lane in that rag of yours, you're going to have to answer to me."

I saw his gaze dart around the office, no doubt looking for his eighty-year-old security man. It didn't matter, I'd said what I needed to, so I let him go.

I started for the door when he called out, "You can't do that. I'll own that candleshop of yours now. You struck me."

"Where's your proof? It's your word against mine."

He looked at the secretary who'd taken my money, but she replied meekly, "I'm sorry, Mr. Klein, I was on the phone with a customer."

There was no one else in the room. I said, "I'd better not see my name mentioned in your paper, either. Do we understand each other?"

"You can't threaten the free press," he said.

"I'm not threatening the newspaper," I said as I stepped closer. He flinched as I approached, but I never laid another finger on him. Instead, I whispered, "I am threatening you, though."

He jumped back at my words. "There, did you hear that? Gladys, I'm talking to you."

She was on the telephone again and held one hand over the mouthpiece. "Sorry, I wasn't listening. Did you need me for something?"

Klein looked exasperated, then stormed back into his office without another word. I noticed Gladys letting a smile slip past her lips before she could rein it back in.

"Thanks," I said.

She smiled brightly at me and said, "I'm sure I don't know what you're thanking me for."

"Guess," I said as I headed for the door.

"Mr. Black," she called out.

I turned, and she motioned me toward her. When I was close to her, she said softly, "Good for you. He's too casual about pushing people around."

"I lost my temper. Believe me, it's something I would normally never do."

She said, "Perhaps you should lose it more often then."

"You might be right," I said as I walked out of the office with the newspaper tucked under my arm. Confrontations usually left me cold and shaking, but after this one, I felt like I could take on the world. Maybe it was because I'd been fighting for what was left of Becka's memory and reputation. I meant what I'd told him, too. If Hank Klein said one derogatory thing about Becka Lane, he was going to have to answer to me. I'd been so furious with his interview ambush that something nagged at the back of my mind, something about the conversation we'd just had. It wasn't so much what he said as it was how he'd said it. I'd heard that voice recently, but for the life of me I couldn't remember where.

Then it hit me.

I knew in my heart who Becka's secret boyfriend had been, the one who'd been trying to get her back.

It was Hank Klein's voice on her answering machine. I might not be able to prove it without the tape, but I had a new lead to go on, one that I wouldn't let go until I found out the truth.

I couldn't wait to get back to River's Edge before I dug the newspaper out. I found a park bench and opened the paper to page 8A, the same sheet Becka had cut. Pulling the folded section from my pocket, I laid it over the paper I'd just bought.

The articles included brief snippets about an indicted congressman, new proposed stalking laws, illegal dumping and an unidentified woman's body discovered in Larkspur Lake. I got chills as I read the last article. Though there was no mention of sleeping pills found in the woman's system, I had to wonder if Becka had an idea about what would happen to her. I cut the section out with the penknife on my keychain and slipped it in my pocket. I'd have to see what Morton could find out about the woman who drowned. Becka might have just managed to lead us to her own killer.

# Seven

I had some time before I had to get back to open the candleshop, so I decided to try to see Cyrus again. Our earlier conversation had disturbed me greatly, and I wasn't about to obey my friend's wishes. Something was going on there, something that just didn't feel right.

I tried the doorknob when I got to his place, but it was locked this time. I rang the bell, and a few seconds later a large, heavyset man wearing a pair of dress pants and a Windbreaker answered the door.

"Help you?" he asked gruffly.

"I'm here to see Cyrus," I said, trying to see past him inside the house.

"He's not accepting visitors," the man said as he started to close the door.

"I'm his friend. Tell him Harrison Black is here to see him."

The man said, "I've got orders about you in particular. You're supposed to go away and not bother him anymore. Do you understand?"

"Just who are you, anyway?"

The man smiled grimly. "I'm the guy between you and this door. Now beat it," he said, then slammed the door in my face.

Why had Cyrus hired this bulldog to watch his front door? I couldn't imagine anyone threatening him, but why else would he put such a formidable barrier up to visitors? I got in the truck and drove around the corner, then parked behind another vehicle that held ladders, buckets and other cleaning equipment. That was one good thing about driving a pickup truck in neighborhoods like this one. I was usually mistaken for a craftsman at work catering to the needs of people who spent more time behind their desks than they did in their homes. It was the modern, too-often told story of suburbia. Bored housewives and working-class folks inhabited those brightly decorated houses that felt empty nonetheless.

I grabbed a clipboard from under the seat and shoved a pencil behind one ear. Markum had taught me that trick. With a clipboard in his hand and a worried look on his face, a man could go just about anywhere without anyone questioning him. I cut through a neighbor's yard and made my way over to Cyrus's house. There had to be something going on in there that someone didn't want the world to know about.

The windows were dirty from accumulated grime. I pulled out my bandana handkerchief and tried to wipe away the dirt. Was that a newly built ramp covering the steps going up from the sunken living room? Blast it all, I couldn't see much of anything. I was still struggling to get a good look inside when a heavy hand landed on my shoulder.

"You don't take no for an answer, do you?"

The clipboard fell out of my hand as I realized it was Cyrus's personal Cerberus, diligently guarding the gate.

"He's my friend," I protested.

"And he's my employer," the man said as he started pushing me toward the front gate.

"How'd you know I was here?" I asked.

"There's new security around the perimeter. I knew you were coming the second you stepped on his land. Don't come back. I won't be so easy on you next time." He gave me a forced shove, and I nearly lost my balance as I stumbled forward. By the time I'd managed to right myself, I saw that I had crossed the property line. The goon retrieved the clipboard, studied it a moment, then threw it at my feet.

I thought about saying something, but I couldn't think of anything appropriate that might help my case. Most likely he was under the impression that he'd won the war, but all I was willing to concede was a single battle. I'd be back—I wasn't sure how yet—but I would slip past him and see my friend. I considered using some of Becka's grand to buy my way past the bulldog, but it wouldn't be right when we'd earmarked that money for looking into Becka's murder. Besides, I wanted to beat him fairly, not pay him off. I'd find a way, sooner or later.

As I drove to At Wick's End, I wondered exactly what had happened to Cyrus. Was he a prisoner to his fears, or was there something more ominous going on there?

I GOT BACK to the candleshop and started on the daily preparations to open it. There was a knock on my door ten minutes till opening, but I'd learned not to ignore those summonses in the past. When I looked up, though, I was surprised to see that Heather was standing outside.

"Hey, what's going on?" I said as I opened the door for her.

Instead of answering, she held up a bouquet of flowers arranged in a coffee cup. It was filled with muted shades of yellows and browns, and there was enough green finery in it to make the contrast apparent.

"What's with that?" I asked, pointing to the bouquet.

"They're for you," she replied.

"I didn't know you cared."

"I didn't buy them, you nit. The floral shop dropped them off with me when they saw you weren't open yet."

I took the arrangement, and said, "Thanks, I appreciate that."

Heather said, "Aren't you even going to read the card?"

"Why, have you seen it already?"

"I resent that, Harrison. I would never do such a thing," she added with a slight smile, "Besides, it was taped shut, and I couldn't figure out how to peek without you knowing it."

I laughed, then said, "Thanks again."

"Okay, but don't expect me to share the next juicy secret I uncover with you."

"It's a deal."

The look of frustration from her denied curiosity as she left would have been worth the price of the bouquet if I'd sent it myself.

I slit the envelope open and retrieved the card. *"Thanks for sharing last night with me. Don't worry, your secret is safe. Erin."* It was a sweet gesture, but I thanked the heavens above that I hadn't read it in front of Heather. There were a thousand things she would have read into that message, and all of them would have been wrong. I put the flowers on the front counter, but tucked the card into my jeans pocket. I wasn't eager to have Eve quiz me, either.

I called Erin's number at work, and she picked up on the first ring. "Thanks for the flowers," I said.

"You don't mind, do you?"

"Why should I mind? I appreciate the gesture."

Erin sighed, then said, "As soon as I ordered them, I started having second thoughts. Most men would be embarrassed to get flowers."

"Well, I'm not one of them. I should have been the one to think of it, though. You did me a lot more good than I did you."

"Don't be so sure of that, Harrison, I needed that talk myself. And I promise, I meant what I said. I'll keep your secret."

"I know you will." A customer knocked on the door, and I glanced at my watch to see that I was thirty seconds past opening. "Listen, I've got an eager candle-maker dying to get in. I'll talk to you later, but I wanted to say thank you."

"You're most welcome," Erin said.

I hung up and unlocked the door. Before I could

flip the sign from CLOSED to OPEN, the man bolted inside.

"May I help you?" I asked.

"I need mold release. I thought I had enough, but I ran out in the middle of a pour."

"You didn't leave the heat on your wax, did you?" I asked as I led him to the spray releases.

"Of course not. What do you think I am, an amateur? I'll take two cans."

I rang up the sale, put his purchases in the bag, then handed it to him. "Thanks for coming by."

He raced for the door. "I don't have much choice, do I? You're the only game in town."

It was customers like that that made me sometimes wish that Belle had left me an emerald mine instead of a candleshop. Mostly, though, I loved the people who shopped At Wick's End.


AFTER HE WAS gone, I looked through the mail and saw a letter from Gary Cragg. He was my attorney of record for River's Edge. The only advantage of having him was his proximity; it was also the biggest disadvantage of the arrangement. I put the letter under the stack of others I had to read and left them on my desk. I'd look through them later. At least there shouldn't be any bills there. They went straight to my accountant, an organized woman named Ann Marie who handled the lion's share of my paperwork for me.

I was just finishing up with another customer when Millie came in carrying a basket of something that smelled like ambrosia. I quickly bagged the woman's purchases and nearly shoved her out the door.

"What is that?" I asked.

"Harrison, I was wondering if you'd mind tasting a new recipe for me."

"Let me grab some cold milk and I'll get right on it. What did you make?"

She pulled the cloth aside and I saw some golden brown muffins. "They have orange slices in them. Try one."

I took a bite, then another, and then the entire muffin was gone. "Wow. Was that nutmeg mixed in with the cinnamon?"

"You're developing quite a palette for baking, aren't you?"

"Hey, as long as you're willing to keep trying new recipes, I'll taste them for you. This batch is a keeper."

"Pooh, I'm beginning to think you're getting too lax. You like everything I bake."

I grinned. "Hey, it's not my fault. If you want a harsh critic, Eve should be here any minute."

"No thanks, I'll stick with your evaluation. Have you decided what you're going to do about Heather and Sanora?"

They were two of my tenants and also my friends. The women had forged a truce the last I'd heard, but I hadn't been at River's Edge as much as I should have been lately. "What's going on with them?"

"They're both threatening to leave," she said simply.

I felt my heart plunge into an ice water bath. "Wait a second. What about their leases? They've both committed to River's Edge."

Millie frowned. "Do you mean to tell me Gary Cragg hasn't spoken with you yet?"

"About what?" Despite how good that orange slice

muffin had been, it suddenly lay in my stomach like concrete.

"He should be the one to tell you. I might get some of the details wrong."

"Come on, Millie, don't do this to me."

She sighed, then said, "Oh, all right, I suppose you have to hear about it sooner or later. According to our lease agreements, any of us can leave River's Edge up to six months after Belle's death. It's been nearly that, and Sanora and Heather are saying that one of them is going to have to go. I'm just afraid you're going to lose them both."

I couldn't stand the thought of my River's Edge family breaking up. "What about you? Are you going to bail out on me, too?"

She frowned. "Harrison Black, you know me better than that. Unless you double my rent, I'm staying."

"What about the rest of the tenants? Come on, Millie, this is no time to be coy. I know everybody in the complex talks to you about everything."

"I'd be offended if I could manage to be convincing. Yes, several folks have already talked to me about the situation."

"So who can I count on, and who's going to leave?"

She said, "Cragg will stay, he's got a fondness for this place, despite how he acts sometimes. I'm here, Suzanne Gladstone's not taking her antique shop anywhere, and you know Markum will stay. The rest are mostly in favor of continuing on, but I'm afraid you're going to lose Heather or Sanora, if not the both of them."

"Blast it all, I thought we got past that."

Millie shrugged. "Sorry to bring bad news to you. If there's anything I can do, just let me know."

"You could broker peace between them," I said.

"Anything but that," she said.

"Coward," I said, smiling.

"I won't deny it. I'd better get back to my café. See you later, Harrison."

"Bye, Millie, and thanks for the snack."

"You're most welcome."

I tried to call Cragg, but either he wasn't answering his telephone or he was out. I dug through the stack of letters on my desk and found the one from him.

I ripped it open and read his brief missive. Millie had stated it clearly enough. I was in danger of losing every tenant I had at River's Edge.

As soon as Eve walked in the door, I said, "Good, you're here. I've got to take care of some things."

"Harrison, are you meddling in Becka's death? Need I remind you that you have a business to run?"

"This *is* business," I said. "I just read Gary Cragg's letter, and I've got to stop Heather and Sanora from moving out."

After I explained the details of the leases with her, she asked, "Well, then why are you standing here? Go speak with them before they both do something you'll regret."

Eve wasn't a big fan of Sanora's, but she and Heather got along fine. Still, she knew as well as I did that River's Edge just barely hung on with full occupancy. Losing two major tenants could be enough to drive me into foreclosure if I couldn't make that monthly mortgage payment.

It was time to see if I could convince them both to stay without resorting to blackmail or threats, though if I had to, I wouldn't hold back.

Not if it meant keeping River's Edge.

# Eight

I wanted to talk to Cragg before I approached either woman, so I hustled up the stairs hoping he'd been screening his calls. He was the only attorney I'd ever heard of who didn't have a secretary/receptionist working the front. Knowing how cheap Cragg was, though, it didn't surprise me.

He was in his office sitting behind his desk, wading through a stack of papers.

"I just called you," I said.

"I chose to ignore it, much as you've been ignoring my requests for a meeting lately."

"In case you hadn't heard, I've kind of been busy, finding old friends dead and things like that." The two of us had gotten off on the wrong foot from the first day we'd met, and our relationship had soured even further since then. If there was one tenant bolting from River's Edge, I wouldn't have shed many tears for Cragg's departure.

His perennially dour expression softened for a moment. "I was sorry to hear about your friend."

"Thanks," I grunted, not really caring for the man's stab at sympathy. "About this letter," I said, waving it in the air.

"I'm familiar with its contents, since I wrote it myself. Harrison, I'm afraid your great-aunt should never have trusted such an incompetent lawyer to draft those leases."

"I'm sure she had her reasons," I said. There was no use discussing it with him. "The question is what are we going to do about it now?"

"I'm afraid there's nothing that can be done. You're going to have to go to each tenant and have every last one of them sign new lease agreements." He slid a stack of papers off one corner of his desk and handed them to me. "You'll see that I've already taken the liberty to sign mine."

I looked at the document and saw that he hadn't decreased his own rent, something I'd been expecting. "I see you've got your current rent listed here."

Cragg nodded. "In exchange for you keeping the rent stabilized for two years at today's level, I will also handle a modicum of legal duties for you, free of charge. Harrison, it's important that you resist the temptation to raise rents throughout the complex, even though legally you have as much right to demand an increase as your tenants do to refuse and leave."

I swear, that thought never even crossed my mind. "I just want things to stay the way they are." I paused, then added, "Honestly though, I'm surprised by what a good deal Belle gave you." I had no idea what the going rate for office space was in the town of Micah's Ridge, but then again, we weren't exactly in the hotbed of the business or legal district.

"Let's just say I want to stay for more reasons than that and leave it."

I knew it wasn't my charming personality that was keeping Gary Cragg at River's Edge, but then I always suspected he had a crush on Sanora. Could it be the lawyer had that big a soft spot for her? His next words left no doubt in my mind. "Our agreement is contingent on you resigning the complete roster of first-floor tenants. Do we understand each other?"

"Oh, yes, there's no doubt about it." So if I lost Sanora or Heather, I'd lose Cragg as well. If I had to hire another attorney to do what he was willing to do free of charge, it might be enough to push me from the black into the red. "I'll do what I can."

"See to it," he said, dismissing me as he dug into his paperwork.

I went back to my apartment for a quick lunch. After all, I was going to need some fortification before I tackled the rest of my tenants.

After a quick bite, I changed my mind about approaching Heather and Sanora first. With the new leases, I decided to take the coward's way out and approach those I thought would resign without much grief. Maybe then if I had every tenant signed but two, I could work something out with my remaining holdouts. In quick order I had Millie signed up again, as well as Suzanne and her antiques, and a handful of the others. By the time five o'clock was approaching, I only had three more signatures to collect. Markum was a shoo-in, but the other two wouldn't be easy.

I decided to tackle Heather first. Her shop, The New

Age, was right next door to mine, and I'd known her since the day I'd moved into River's Edge. She'd been my first friend at the complex, and I couldn't imagine the place without her. There were crystals dangling over the front door when I walked in, and I liked they way they announced each new arrival.

Heather was behind the cash register, frowning as she stroked Esmeralda, her cat and my sometime roommate. Esme lifted her head just as Heather did when I walked in, and they looked at me with the exact same expression on their faces.

"Hey, I'm not the enemy," I said.

I offered Esme my hand, and she rubbed her head against it. At least the cat and I were still on speaking terms.

"You know you're not the one I'm mad at, Harrison." Almost as an afterthought, she added, "I don't know if I told you, but I'm so sorry about Becka."

"Thanks." I had the lease tucked away in my back pocket. "I heard you were threatening to leave. What's going on between you and Sanora?"

"Believe me, you don't want to get into the middle of this. It doesn't concern anyone but us."

"Well, I don't have much choice, because I don't want to lose either one of you."

She looked surprised. "I know the grapevine around here is pretty fast, but this is ridiculous."

"Heather, ordinarily I'd respect your wishes and butt out, but with this lease mix-up, I'm involved." I pulled the agreement out of my pocket and shoved it toward her. "Would you sign this? As a favor to me? I don't want to lose you."

She looked at the lease like a mobster eyeing a subpoena. "Did she sign one?"

"I haven't talked to her yet," I said. "I've known you longer, but I don't want to take sides here. I came to you first, though. That's got to count for something."

She said, "Harrison, maybe it's time I moved on. This might just be a sign."

I knew Heather believed in signs, omens and portents, so it was nothing to scoff at. "The only thing it's a sign of is the incompetence of the lawyer who drew it up. I don't want to run River's Edge without you."

Heather looked touched by the declaration, but stood her ground. "I can't imagine going another two years with that woman at the other end of the complex."

"At least tell me what this latest scuffle is about."

"If you want to know, ask her." Heather hesitated, then added, "Harrison, what happened to her probation? You can refuse to renew her lease if you wanted to."

"That's just it. She hasn't given me the slightest cause to throw her out. Sanora belongs here, too."

"I should have known you'd say that," Heather said huffily.

Esme looked at her owner, then at me. She sneezed once, then jumped off the counter and landed with fluid grace. Her tail held proudly in the air, she showed us both what she thought of us at the moment.

Heather said, "Now if you'll excuse me, I'm two dollars and thirty seven cents over, and I'm not leaving until my books balance."

I tucked the lease back in my pocket and left her with her accounting problem. Hopefully I'd have better luck with Sanora. I surely couldn't have any less.

She was throwing at her pottery wheel when I walked into The Pot Shot.

Instead of Heather's scowl, Sanora greeted me with a broad smile. "Harrison, it's good to see you out and about. How are you holding up?"

"I'm doing better," I said. "But that's not why I'm here."

Her smile dimmed. "Then I don't want to talk about it." The tension in her voice was obvious as the vase she was turning suddenly collapsed under the pressure of her hands.

"Sorry, I hope I didn't cause that," I said.

She scraped the clay off the wheel. "It happens."

After Sanora washed her hands, she dried them with a towel. I offered her the lease, but she wouldn't touch it.

"Is there any chance you'll sign this without a fuss?"

"Now what do you think," she said as she brushed past me.

"I think you're both making this harder than it has to be."

Sanora said, "I can't help you there. If Heather signs, let me know so I can start looking for another place."

"Blast it, woman, she won't even tell me what's wrong. I suppose you're mute on the subject as well."

"Harrison, I'll tell you anything you want to know. The problem's with her, not me."

I said, "Go ahead then, enlighten me."

At that moment, a young woman came into the shop. "Excuse me. I'm looking for a dozen wedding gifts for my bridal party. Can you help me?"

Sanora said, "Absolutely, ma'am." She turned to me and added, "We'll finish this later."

The bride-to-be said, "I'm not interrupting anything, am I? I can always come back. There are so many neat places in this complex. I can't believe I never heard of it before."

"Please, don't go on my account," I said quickly. "I was just leaving."

Sanora mouthed a thank-you toward me, but she needn't have. No matter how badly I wanted to know the source of the latest conflict between my tenants, the customer had to always come first. If Sanora had the opportunity to sell a dozen different pieces in one shot, I couldn't interfere with that. I'd just have to be patient and wait until she could enlighten me. There was nothing left for me to do but to go back to the candleshop and see if I could make a sale like Sanora's.

No such luck. Eve and I sold enough supplies over the course of the rest of the day to pay our wages, but just barely. As to the lighting bill, well, we were going to have to rely on another day's sales to do that. I kept watching the door throughout the afternoon, expecting to see Sanora every time it opened, but by the end of the day I'd just about given up on her. When the door chime announced a visitor ten minutes before closing, I just knew it had to be her.

"Oh, it's you," I said as Markum walked into At Wick's End.

"Well, I have to say, I've had warmer welcomes in my life."

"Sorry, I was hoping Sanora would come by today."

He said, "I hope it wasn't important. I just saw her drive off."

I drummed my fingers on the counter. "The thing is, it *was* important."

"Does this have anything to do with what we've been working on?"

"No, it's about something else, but I still need to speak with her. Don't worry about it. It can probably wait until tomorrow. So what's up with you?"

He looked sideways at Eve, then said, "I was hoping you were free. We need to talk."

I suddenly remembered Markum's unsigned lease upstairs still sitting on my end table. "Yeah, I need to talk to you, too. Can you give me half an hour? I've got to finish up here."

"That's fine," Markum said. "I'll be at Millie's. Come by when you're finished."

"I will," I promised, and the big man left.

After he was gone, Eve said, "You two are as thick as thieves these days, aren't you?"

"We're friends, if that's what you mean." Ordinarily I went out of my way to avoid angering Eve about anything, but I didn't care for her tone whenever she spoke about Markum.

"I'm not at all certain Belle would be pleased with your friendship. I daresay she wouldn't have approved at all."

"My great-aunt rented him office space," I said. "That's all the blessing I need."

"It's your business," she said curtly.

"Yes, it is," I replied, with just as much frost in my voice as she'd had in hers.

Eve took my tone in, then looked at the clock. "If you'll excuse me, I believe I'll be leaving early today."

I knew I'd done it, but there was no backing down now. After all, At Wick's End belonged to me; me and the bank, at any rate. I knew from past experience how

Eve behaved when I offended her, but at that moment, I didn't care how she felt.

Eve looked absolutely startled by my reply, but she couldn't back down either. She grabbed her jacket, then left without saying good-bye. It was doubtful whether she'd bother coming in the next day, but I was tired of constantly tiptoeing around her. I'd learned enough during my time working at the candleshop to run the place solo, though I wasn't at all eager to do it by myself. The point was, I could if I had to, something I wouldn't have been able to say in the past. I was finally starting to consider myself a candlemaker, by vocation as well as avocation.

At least it was peaceful as I ran my reports off the register and balanced the till. I decided to let the deposit wait until the next morning before work. I had too much on my mind to bother with it at the moment. I turned off the lights, locked the door to the candleshop, then walked over to Millie's to see what Markum had uncovered since we'd last spoke. I glanced into Heather's shop as I walked past it, but the CLOSED sign was up and all the lights were out.

I was at the door of The Crocked Pot when Pearly Gray stopped me before I could walk inside. "Harrison, may I trouble you for a moment?"

I looked through the glass and saw Markum watching us. I held up one finger, and he nodded.

I turned back to Pearly and said, "Go ahead, what's on your mind?"

"Actually, it's about Sanora and Heather. Have you heard about the spat they're having?"

"Yes, it's just come to my attention. I haven't been able to figure out what they're fighting about, let alone work on some kind of resolution. It's a real mess. Do you happen to know what this is all about?"

"No, I've been reluctant up to this point to interfere, but it's important we stop this before it has the opportunity to escalate. As you know, I've had some modicum of success in the past helping people resolve their issues with one another. I think I can help them in a private session."

I knew Pearly had worked as a very successful psychologist before becoming the River's Edge handyman in his "retirement," but his suggestion still managed to startle me. "Are you saying you want them to go into couple's therapy?"

"I'm thinking more along the lines of a conflict-resolution approach," he said.

I patted his shoulder. "Pearly, you can call it whatever you'd like if you can get them both to stay at River's Edge."

"Excellent," Pearly said, the gleam in his eyes growing sharper. "Thank you, Harrison."

"Don't thank me," I said, "I don't want any of the credit for this, or any blame, for that matter. Just let me know how you do."

"Absolutely," he said, already lost in planning his approach to the volatile situation. I could tell that Pearly was eager to speak with the women in a professional capacity, though he'd been retired for some time. If he could patch things up between Heather and Sanora, he would be a miracle worker. And the best thing about it was that I wasn't directly involved with the problem, at least for the time being.

I walked into The Crocked Pot and asked Millie, "How about a cup of coffee? Tell you what, why don't you surprise me with the blend?" Millie loved it when

I was feeling adventurous. I added, "No more of those strong caffeine surprises, though. It took me three days to get to sleep the last time you mixed me one of your specialties."

"It will be something gentle, I promise."

"Are there any more of those orange-slice muffins in back?"

"Sorry, they're all gone. But I'm making a fresh batch in the morning."

I considered my waistline, then denied the direct evidence to the contrary that I needed to cut back. "Save three or four for me," I said.

"You can have two," she said, but I saw the dimples blossom on her cheeks.

I joined Markum and took a sip of coffee. Millie had kept her word; it was a gentle, nutty blend that I really liked. I said to him, "Sorry about that. Pearly cornered me before I could get inside."

"No problem, Harrison. Was it River's Edge business?"

I nodded, but didn't elaborate. The last thing I wanted to do was air our dirty laundry with customers around.

He accepted it at face value. "Any chance you could get that coffee to go? We've got a lot to talk about it, and I'm not sure this is the right place for it."

"Sure thing," I said, standing up and sipping the coffee. Millie let me take her mugs with me, as long as I brought them back by the next morning so they could be washed and put into circulation again. "You want to go to my apartment or your office?"

"Let's go to my office," he said. "There's something there I want to show you."

We walked upstairs together, but I stopped at my

apartment door before we got to his office. "I'll just be a second."

I went in, moved the deposit pouch from under my arm to under the couch, then retrieved Markum's lease. The deposit would have been better off in the bank, or even in somebody's safe, but my hiding place under the couch would be fine until I could take it in the morning. I'd made a mistake with a deposit when I'd first taken over At Wick's End by leaving it in my truck, but that had never happened again. I'd learned that particular lesson all too well.

I tucked the lease in my back pocket and walked down the hall to Markum's office. The travel posters on the walls had changed since I'd been there last. For a man who spent so much of his time in exotic locales, he never seemed to grow tired of the vistas of faraway lands.

I took the lease out and slid it across the desk toward him.

"What's this?" he asked.

"Didn't you get Cragg's letter? Everyone else in the building got one."

"Oh, you mean the one about the lease?" He edged the document back across the desk toward me with the butt of his pen. "Are you sure you want to renew my option here? I know how some of the folks at River's Edge feel about my presence."

"Just sign it, Markum. I'm having enough trouble with Heather and Sanora. I don't need any from you."

He smiled as he uncapped his pen, then signed his name with a flourish. I took the lease back, folded it and stuck it back in my pocket. "Now that we've got that out of the way, what did you find out?"

# Nine

"THERE'S really no easy way to tell you this," Markum said. "I found out who Becka was seeing."

"It was Hank Klein, the newspaper guy," I said flatly.

Markum sat up in his chair. "Now how in creation did you come up with that? It took me most of the day to figure it out, and I had to call in half a dozen favors to do it."

I felt guilty about not sharing what I'd discovered, but there was nothing I could do about it now. "It was sheer dumb luck," I admitted. "I heard him talking this morning when I dropped in to get a newspaper. It clicked that his voice was the one on Becka's answering machine."

Markum nodded. "I feel better about it, then. We've got two sources that are giving us the same answer."

"We're not reporters working on a story. I don't care if we have verification or not."

Markum said, "Harrison, I've been meaning to talk to you about that. I know you're taking this personally, there's no way you couldn't, but don't let that interfere with what we're doing. Have you thought about how we're going to handle the situation once we find out who killed Becka?"

"That's easy. We tell Sheriff Morton."

"Do you honestly think he's going to believe us? We might not exactly have proof that would stand up in court, do you understand what I'm trying to tell you?"

I felt a cold chill sweep through me. "What are you suggesting, that we punish the killer ourselves?"

"It happens more often than you might think," he said.

I stood up. "I don't like the way this conversation is heading."

"It's something we need to consider, that's all I'm saying."

"I don't have to like it, though, do I?" I walked out of his office, barely acknowledging his good night on my way out. Did he mean what I thought he did? Was Markum suggesting we punish the offender ourselves? It was too much for me to take. I went back to my apartment, added Markum's lease to the others I had, then I double-dead-bolted my door.

For tonight, I wanted to be alone with my thoughts. Esme herself wouldn't have been welcome. As I cleaned out my pockets, I found the article I'd cut out of the newspaper. I'd forgotten to share it with Markum, but I was in no mood to even be in the same room with him at the moment. I put it on my dresser and did my best to forget about what I'd just heard from my best friend.

I'd just settled down with a Charlotte MacLeod novel I'd never read when there was a knock on my door. I wasn't in the mood to see anyone, and I thought about pretending I wasn't there.

"Harrison? Are you there?"

It was the sheriff. He was one person I couldn't afford to ignore.

I opened the door. "Come on in."

He stepped past me, his hat in hand, and said, "Sorry it's so late, but I need to talk to you about a few things."

"Did you find anything out about Becka?"

"No, as far as I'm concerned, there's nothing to talk about there." He spun his sheriff's hat in his hands, a sure sign he was unhappy about something. "First, the woman you asked me about who drowned in Larkspur Lake. They found her fishing boat this morning. Evidently she tripped and fell off. The coroner says she hit her head as she went overboard."

"Or maybe somebody hit her over the head, then tossed her over the side."

"Harrison, stop looking for conspiracies and cover-ups everywhere. It was an accident."

"Maybe. What else did you want to talk to me about?"

"We need to discuss the situation with Cyrus."

That got my attention. "What about him? Is he all right?"

Morton said, "Slow down. He's fine, as far as I can tell. He wants you to leave him alone." The words rushed out, and I could tell how much the sheriff hated having to say them.

"Wait a second, let me get this straight. You're here to give me a message like that? You've got to be kidding."

His glare burned right through me. "Does it look like I'm kidding? If you bother him anymore, he told me to tell you that he'll press charges for trespassing and stalking and harassment and anything else I can come up with. Harrison, the man's old and he's tired. Leave him alone."

I couldn't believe what I was hearing. "Morton, we've been friends since I took over this place, at least I thought we were. Runion started sniffing around Cyrus's land and I went to see him. The first time I was there he wouldn't come out and face me. When I came back the next time, he had some kind of bodyguard at the door. I don't get it."

"He doesn't want to see you, or anyone else. Don't take it personally, Harrison, the guy's allowed to be a little eccentric, as old and as rich as he is."

Morton started for the door, but I stepped in his way. "Did you see him face-to-face? I just want to know that he's all right."

The sheriff looked annoyed. "No, he called me on the phone. I'm doing this for you as much as I am for him. He's serious, Harrison."

It wasn't good enough for me, though. "So he picks up the telephone and you hop right over here. He's got you trained pretty well, doesn't he?"

I saw Morton's jaw tighten and realized I'd pushed the sheriff too far with my last comment. He took a few seconds, gathered his calm, then said, "You've had a rough couple of days, so I'm going to let that slide." He headed for the door again, and this time I stepped out of his way. Morton was just about to leave when he turned back to me and said, "Cyrus and my daddy used to be fishing buddies. I've known that man my entire life, and you should know that I'd crawl through glass for him."

"Then you should be as concerned as I am about him," I said.

"Leave him alone, Harrison."

Then the sheriff was gone.

I took Morton's warning seriously, but I wasn't going to give up on my friend. Cyrus's behavior couldn't be passed off as an old man's eccentricity. He'd been scared about something when I'd visited him, and if Morton wasn't willing to look into it, I was going to have to add it to my list.

I WAS AT Millie's the next day for breakfast, collecting my orange slice muffins, when I saw Markum sitting alone in one corner of the café. It was the earliest I'd ever seen him awake, and I had to make up my mind in a heartbeat how I was going to handle being around him after what we'd talked about the night before.

I decided he was too good a friend to lose over what had been said. I walked straight to his table and said, "I didn't think your alarm clock worked this early." I added a smile to take the edge off my words.

He looked relieved when I said it. "If you want to know the truth, I haven't been to bed yet."

I tapped his cup. "Here's a tip. If you're trying to beat insomnia, coffee's not going to be much help."

He laughed as he scooted out the chair across from him. "Sit down."

"I'll be right back," I said.

Millie was at the counter with a pair of orange slice muffins on a plate. I said, "Hey, I thought we agreed on three."

She smiled. "Good morning to you, too, Harrison."

"Hi, Millie. So what happened to my third muffin?"

She pulled the plate back. "Honestly, I'm beginning to think you should just get one."

I grabbed it before she could slide the treats completely out of my reach. "Two sound great. Any chance I can get some cold milk to go with these?"

"I've got a glass chilling in the freezer for you. It should be icy by now."

I took the milk and saw it had a crust of white ice across its top. "Thanks, it's perfect."

She said, "I don't know how you can drink it that cold. It would shatter my teeth if I tried it."

"This is the only way to drink milk," I said. I took the glass and the plate of muffins to Markum's table. He shuddered when he saw what I had.

"I haven't had a glass of milk since I was nine," he said. "Millie'd better do something about that refrigerator, it's got to be broken."

"She had this in the freezer for me," I said, not explaining my preference.

He didn't comment, which was something I liked about Markum. The man knew when to let something go and when to pursue it. We chatted as we ate, and just about the only thing we didn't discuss was Becka Lane. It was as if the last two days hadn't happened at all. The orange slice muffins were even better than I'd remembered, and when I'd finished my second, I was looking at Millie, hoping she'd have a third waiting for me. No such luck. I was turning into a real bakery glutton being around her, so I decided to stop at two. The fact that Millie wouldn't let me have a third helped me hold to my resolve.

I cleaned up the table and said, "If you've got some time, we can finish what we started last night."

He looked surprised. "I thought you had a candleshop to run."

I glanced at the clock over Millie's counter and said, "I've got an hour before I have to be there. Do you have the time and the energy, or would you rather do it later?"

He stood. "Now's as good a time as any."

As we walked upstairs to his office, I said, "When do you think we should confront Klein?"

"Not yet. I want to cover everything else we've got before I tackle him. I did talk to Runion about your other trouble with your friend Cyrus."

As we walked into Markum's office, I took my seat across from his desk and asked, "Did you have any luck with him?" I wasn't going to mention the source of our tension the night before, and if I knew Markum, he wasn't about to bring it up either.

"The man's as slippery as a snake oil salesman and has the constitution of one to boot. I got him to admit a few things before he clammed up, though."

I didn't doubt Markum would be able to find a way around Runion's reticence. "What did he say?"

"He's got big plans for the piece of land next to yours, and from the way he swaggered around his office, it's close to a done deal. I was trying to break the ice with him, posing as a possible investor. I figured to discuss his schemes a little before I brought Becka's name into the conversation. If there's one thing a rooster likes to do, it's strut."

"So what happened after you brought Becka's name up? Could he explain why she had his phone number in her purse?"

Markum frowned. "He clammed up in a heartbeat, and it was all he could do to keep from throwing me out of his office. Harrison, I've been wondering if we're wrong about Klein being Becka's secret boyfriend, despite what we first thought."

"What do you mean?"

Markum said, "We were both pretty convinced that it was Klein's voice on the tape, but I'm not so sure anymore. I found myself wondering if Runion's voice could have been a match as well as Klein's, and I'm sorry to say I couldn't rule out either one of them."

"You had your other source, too."

"One that turned out to be less reliable than I first thought." He shook his head. "Don't forget, Becka did have Runion's telephone number in her purse. That's got to mean something."

"She wouldn't have to write her boyfriend's number down to remember it, would she?"

Markum frowned, stood, then stared at a poster of Bali. "If the relationship was new enough, maybe she did. I'm afraid we can't rule him out."

"So she was either sleeping with a muckraking married newspaper publisher or a sleazy developer. It doesn't speak well of Becka's taste in men, does it?"

"You can't judge her, Harrison, she's beyond that. Remember, she broke up with whoever it was she'd been seeing. The question is, why? If it was Klein, did she dump him because he was married? If Runion was the man, maybe she stumbled across something he was doing, something she couldn't live with."

"So instead of getting clearer, we've managed to muddy the water more."

He frowned and ran his hands through his unruly black hair. "I admit it's more complicated than I first thought. Don't worry, though, we're not finished yet." He stifled a yawn, then said, "Excuse me."

"Listen, why don't you see if you can catch a nap? I've got to open the candleshop in ten minutes, and we can't do anything at the moment."

He nodded. "I think I will. If you need me, call. Don't worry about waking me up."

"Do you want to use my couch for your nap? I don't mind." I paused, then added, "I'd offer you my bed, but I don't have any clean sheets on hand."

He slapped my shoulder with a meaty hand. "Thanks for the offer, but I'm going to head home. Remember, call me if anything occurs to you. I can't help but think we're missing something."

Markum locked his office behind us and we parted company outside.

I saw Heather leaving her shop, an odd thing to be happening ten minutes before opening, but she met my greeting with a sharp wave of her hand and scampered past me as she hurried to The Crocked Pot. I hoped Pearly had better luck than I had resolving the conflict my tenants were putting us all through. I didn't want to face too many more days in the midst of Heather's and Sanora's feud. If I didn't desperately want them both at River's Edge, I was tempted to let them battle it out, with the loser leaving the complex forever. After Heather was gone, I walked to At Wick's End and started to put my key in the lock.

That's when I realized that it was already open.

Someone had gotten to my candleshop before me, but I knew Eve wasn't scheduled to come in until noon.

That left a dozen possible reasons why At Wick's End was open, and none of them were good.

# Ten

"WHO'S there?" I called out as I walked into At Wick's End. I probably should have called Morton before going inside, but blast it all, that candleshop belonged to me.

"I've got a gun," I said, for some insanely irrational reason.

"Then I certainly hope the safety's on," a cultured voice called out from back. I felt my heart settle back down as Pearly stepped out of the shadows.

"What are you doing here in the dark?" I asked as I flipped on the main bank of lights. Nothing happened.

"You asked me to replace the light switch in back, remember? I was forced to cut the breaker for the entire store because whoever installed the fuse box left some sketchy notes that are impossible to decipher."

"That's fine. Sorry about the threat."

He laughed. "You were quite convincing, actually. I found myself fighting the urge to come out with my hands up." He tossed a switch in his hand and said, "I've replaced the culprit, so as soon as I can reengage the fuse box, you'll have power again, and a working switch as well."

"Thanks, Pearly," I said. "Have you had a chance to speak with Heather and Sanora yet?"

"No, but I've got them on my schedule. I have high hopes, Harrison."

"Listen, don't take it as a personal insult if you can't work things out between them," I said as I walked him to the door.

"You should have more faith in me than that," he said, a smile on his lips.

"I'm just saying that their history runs hot and deep. Keep that in mind."

He patted my shoulder gently. "Thank you for your concern."

Three minutes later the overhead lights came on and I had power in the candleshop again. I just hoped Pearly would be as successful when he talked to Heather and Sanora.

It was a busy morning, and I was happy for the distractions of selling candlemaking supplies to the public. The more I worked in At Wick's End, the larger my list of customers grew, and more importantly, the bigger my circle of friends. I knew folks who traveled in all walks of life. When my great-aunt left me River's Edge, I never dreamed she'd be changing my life so much. I still had her letter in a simple frame upstairs, the one where she'd first told me I was about to inherit the complex. I could remember reading it in the lawyer's office, amazed by the scope of what Belle was suggesting.

The most important words she'd given me were when she'd said, *"Candles bring light into the world, my boy, and we need all the illumination we can get."* I tried to live up to those words every day.

A middle-aged woman came into the shop and went directly to the mold releases. If she'd been in the store before, I hadn't noticed her.

"Can I help you?" I asked.

She looked at me through squinted eyes. "I don't know, can you? I assume you are willing to assist me, since you appear to be working in this establishment, but that is the question, isn't it? Can you help me?"

"I surely hope so," I said, not sure what I was getting myself into. "Do you need some release?"

"I do indeed. Belle Black, the proprietress here and the woman I assume is your immediate superior, used to carry a product in a gray and red can, but I'm afraid I've forgotten the name of it."

I said, "You're looking for Yukon Release." I handed her a can, then said, "They changed the label, but the product's still the same. Will there be anything else?"

She looked around the store, then said, "I was hoping to spend a moment or two chatting with Belle. I've been touring Australia. She'd yearned to go with me, but I'm afraid her finances and commitments here limited her traveling." She patted her handbag and said, "I've brought her a souvenir I know she'll absolutely adore."

I hadn't had to tell any customers about my great-aunt's demise in months, and I was finally hoping I wouldn't have to anymore. Belle was loved by a great many people, and I hadn't found an easy way to pass the news on, despite countless times to practice.

"I'm sorry to have to tell you this, but she died while

you were away," I said, not wanting to go into details unless I was pressed.

"Oh, dear. That's dreadful," the woman said as she stumbled back against a shelf full of votive molds. "Was it her heart?"

I shook my head. "I'm afraid it was more ominous than that. She was killed here in the candleshop."

"That is ghastly," the woman said. "And you're the new owner? Did Eve leave you as well?"

"I'm the owner, but Eve's still here. I'm Harrison Black," I said as I offered her my hand.

"Candace Grishaber," she said. It took her a moment, then she added, "Black, did you say? Were you related to Belle?"

"She was my great-aunt," I said.

"And she was my great friend," she said. "I'll miss her."

"As do I," I said. I couldn't bear the thought of spending any more time dwelling on the past. It left me sad and empty inside, and it did nothing to bring Belle's memory back. "Are you done?"

She arched one eyebrow. "I suppose if I were a turkey I might be done. As it is though, I am human, therefore I am finished."

I started to reply when she said, "Forgive a retired English teacher. We never quite get over correcting our students."

"You're forgiven," I said as I rang up her purchase. "I hope you visit again."

"You can count on it, my dear young man."

Eve walked in for her shift ten minutes after Ms. Grishaber had gone. When I told her about the visit, Eve said, "Belle really did want to go with Candace, but she couldn't swing it. I told her it was just as well. The woman's fussbudgeting would have driven her crazy inside a week. No, that's not fair; Belle would have found it charming. On the other hand, I would have shoved her out of the jet before we even took off."

She glanced at the report I ran midday and said, "You've been busy, haven't you?"

"It's been steady. Eve, I hate to ask, but could you watch the place for me this afternoon? There are a few more things I need to take care of."

"Harrison Black, are you sticking your nose in where it doesn't belong?"

"That's a matter of opinion, I guess."

Eve studied me a second, then said, "Try not to get arrested, would you? I don't think the candleshop could take any more negative publicity."

"I'll try, but I can't make any promises," I said.

In all honesty, there was something besides looking into Becka's murder that I needed to do at the moment. I wasn't about to give up on my friend Cyrus, no matter what Morton had said. There had to be a way around that guard, and I knew in my heart that if I could get Cyrus to talk to me, we could straighten this all out.

Either that or I might be spending the night in one of only two jail cells in all of Micah's Ridge.

DESPITE MY GOOD intentions, I never even got close to Cyrus. The driveway was blocked off with sawhorses, and a different, tougher-looking man was standing patrol just inside the property. From my earlier confrontation, I knew that the perimeter was wired, so there was no getting in that way. I was going to have to rely on

Sheriff Morton to find out what was happening with my friend.

My stomach grumbled and I realized I'd forgotten all about lunch. I didn't want to head back to River's Edge; Eve might see me there and expect me to work. Instead, I drove to A Slice of Heaven for some pizza and a Coke. April May was behind the counter, running a report on her cash register.

"Any chance I could get a slice?" I asked.

"Absolutely. I'm just checking my numbers. I've got a new girl on the register," she said in a softer voice, "and since she started, the totals just don't add up."

"Do you think she's stealing from you?"

April shook her head. "No, it's more likely she's having trouble making change. I'm going to have a talk with her, but I wanted something to back it up, so she ran the register by herself for the lunch rush." She studied the tape, then said, "I already checked the till. It's worse than I thought."

"Is there a lot missing?"

She shook her head. "That I could live with if I had to, but I've got twenty-seven dollars and seventeen cents that don't belong to me." She shrugged, then said, "This isn't going to be pretty. Let me get your slice started."

After she slid one into the oven to reheat, I said, "I'd ask you to join me, but it sounds like you've got a mess on your hands."

"If she was anybody else I could just fire her, but she happens to be my best friend's daughter. I'm not sure what I'm going to do, but I know one thing. She's worked her last shift at the register."

I decided to hang out by the counter since the lunch

crowd was gone. April grabbed my Coke, then said, "Shouldn't you be selling candles or something?"

"Probably, but I'm working on something and I can't stop."

She nodded. "You're looking for your friend Becka's killer, aren't you?"

"Now how in the world did you know that?" I knew Micah's Ridge was small, but the grapevine could be eerie at times.

"I overheard something here last night. Folks are talking about you, how you found the body and took it upon yourself to investigate. Harrison, you've been asking questions around town. People are bound to talk."

"Well, I wish I could deny it, but it's all true. I don't buy the theory that Becka overdosed for a second. She hated pills. I just wish I had something more to go on."

April looked around her restaurant, though there was no one within twenty feet of us. "Have you looked around for a boyfriend?"

"I've tried. I've come up with a couple of leads, but nothing I can be sure of."

April wiped the counter down, or at least pretended to. "Two weeks ago she was in here with a man it shocked me to see her with."

"Who was it?"

"Do you know Greg Runion?"

"I've had the misfortune to deal with him a time or two in the past. Did they come here on a date?"

"I don't know if you could call it a date," she said. "They were arguing about something, and she left in a huff. Funny thing is, just outside she ran into Hank Klein, and they started arguing, too." She added, "Hang on a second. Let me get that slice for you."

A young woman with long red hair pulled back into a ponytail approached April and asked, "You wanted to see me?"

"Hang on a second, let me take care of this customer."

"Would you like me to ring the sale up?" she asked eagerly.

"No, it's already taken care of."

April slid the pizza across to me, then nudged me away from the counter with a single look.

I took the pizza, grabbed my Coke and sat at one of the tables near the jukebox. I wasn't in the mood for music with my meal, though. As I ate the slice, I kept thinking about what an odd combination Runion and Becka made. Markum was starting to believe that it could have been Runion's voice we'd heard on Becka's answering machine, but I was still positive it was Klein's.

After I ate, I had some time to kill before I went back to the candleshop, so I decided to pay a visit to Runion and see if he'd deny what April had just told me. Markum was convinced that Runion could be Becka's secret boyfriend, but even with what April had just told me, I couldn't see it. Still, I wanted to hear his voice again in person to see if I could compare it with the man on the answering machine. I'd deal with Markum later. The last thing he needed was to lose any more sleep over this.

Runion's secretary Jeanie was behind her desk, and she greeted me with a smile when I walked in. "If it isn't Harrison Black. How are you this fine day?" Her Tennessee accent melted as she spoke, her voice filled with different inflections from the ones found in my part of North Carolina.

"I'm fine, Jeanie, how are you?"

"I'm so healthy I could crow."

"That's good to hear. Is your boss in?"

Her smile dimmed. "Greg's back there, but I should warn you, he's been in a bear of a mood lately."

I lowered my voice and asked, "Could I ask you something?"

"Anything," Jeanie said.

"Is there a chance Runion's had a secret girlfriend over the last few months?"

Jeanie frowned. "Do you mean just one? He fancies himself a lady's man, and evidently there *are* some women attracted to the slick, greasy type."

Runion came out of his office. "Jeanie, who are you talking to?" He spotted me and said, "Black, what are you doing here? I thought we were through talking." It was obvious he wasn't trying to sell me anything, or buy anything from me, either. I was getting the real Greg Runion, an ugly face he kept well hidden from the rest of the world. "If this is about buying Cyrus Walters's land, you're wasting your breath."

"How do you know I didn't come by to break Belle's will like you asked me to?"

That got his attention. "Let's talk, then. Come on into my office. Jeanie, hold my calls." He paused at the door, then added, "Unless it's Sam Ridgway."

Runion thought a second, then added, "I'm waiting to hear from Dale James, too. You know what, I'll take whoever calls."

My number-one status was dropping precipitously as he walked in behind me.

He sat behind his expansive desk and said, "Now what's it going to take to get you to break that agreement?"

"First you have to answer some of my questions, and I want the truth."

He looked startled, but nodded. "Fire away."

"Have you been dating Becka Lane recently?"

A cloud crossed his brow. "Harrison, I'm a single man. I date a lot of women in the course of a year."

"I'm talking about a few weeks ago. Your memory should be clear on that." I added, "Don't bother denying it, someone saw you two out a few weeks ago."

Runion reluctantly admitted, "We might have had dinner a time or two, but we weren't dating. In fact, she turned me down the last time I asked her out. Turns out she was seeing somebody new."

"Why should I believe you?" I asked.

"Harrison, frankly I don't give a rat's tail if you do or not." He studied me a moment, then said, "You have no intention of selling out, do you? You know what? I don't need your land anymore. I've got another piece of property all but sewn up."

"Did you have anything to do with the guards at Cyrus's place? I can't get in to see him."

Runion didn't look surprised by the news, but I wasn't sure that meant anything. "The old man's got guards now? Maybe he just wants his privacy."

"And maybe he's a prisoner in his own house."

Runion laughed at the accusation. "Sure, that's it. I've got the old man sewn up tighter than a bug in his own place. Harrison, you've got a good imagination there, boy. Now kindly clear out of my office, I've got serious work to do. Go make a candle or something."

I got up, leaving his door open as I left. He called to Jeanie, "After you see Mr. Black out, come in here and take a letter."

I told Jeanie, "You don't have to walk me out, I'm leaving."

She got up anyway. "I need to stretch my legs." Jeanie surprised me by walking out to the sidewalk with me. When we were outside, she said, "He's doing something with Cyrus, and it's shady, if you ask me. Be careful."

"I will. Thanks for the warning."

"You don't understand. Harrison, I know Greg acts like a jerk, but he's worse than you think. He's gotten tied up with some folks who are nothing but trouble, and I'd hate to see you get hurt."

"I'm not backing down, Jeanie. Cyrus Walters is a friend of mine, and I don't let my friends down."

She touched my arm. "I know how you are, I've heard about your streak of nobility. I'm just saying you should watch your back."

"I plan to."

I started to walk off when Jeanie called out, "So, is it fun making candles?"

"You should come by At Wick's End. I'll give you a candlemaking lesson, on the house."

She smiled. "I appreciate the offer, but I pay my own way, Harrison. I might really come by, though."

"You're always welcome there, you know that."

The office door opened and Runion stuck his head out. "I didn't ask you to walk him to his car. Come on, we've got work to do."

"I'll be there in a minute," she said.

Runion obviously considered arguing the point, then he saw the severe crease on her brow. After her boss was gone, Jeanie said, "I'll keep my ears open. If I hear anything about Becka or Cyrus, I'll let you know."

"Thanks, I do appreciate that. Jeanie, is it safe for you to cross Runion like this? I don't want you to take any chances on my account."

"It's sweet of you to ask, but I'll be fine. I had better get back in there, though. I've pushed him enough today. Bye, Harrison."

"Good-bye."

As I drove back to River's Edge, I felt happier than I had since I'd found Becka's body. With Jeanie spying for me on the inside, I didn't have to confront Runion anymore.

Still, there had to be something I could do about Cyrus.

I was halfway back to River's Edge when it hit me.

Suddenly I knew exactly what I had to do.

# Eleven

As soon as I got back to River's Edge, I raced upstairs to check the telephone book. There was one person I knew who would give me the information I was after. I just hoped she was working today.

Frannie Wilson answered on the third ring. "Registrar of Deeds," she said efficiently.

"Frannie, this is Harrison Black. I need a favor."

Frannie laughed. "That's the only reason you ever call, isn't it? The last time you needed a favor, you at least dragged your hind-end down to my office."

"I would have visited you, but this is kind of urgent. Do you know how I can get hold of Ruth Nash?"

Frannie thought a moment, then said, "Harrison, why are you looking for Cyrus's sister? I heard he was giving you the brush-off, and I'm not all that eager to make that family mad at me. Is Cyrus really trying to keep you from visiting him?"

"Me and everyone else in Micah's Ridge. Frannie,

something's wrong, I just don't know what it is. Cyrus has two guards out in front of his house to keep folks away. Does that sound like the man you know?"

"No," she admitted. "That's odd, even for Cyrus. So you're going to bring in the big gun, huh? Yes, I suppose it's merited. One thing, though, Harrison. If Cyrus is through with you, I want you to promise me you'll drop this."

"I give you my word. I just want to make sure he's all right."

"Then I'll give you Ruth's number." After she read it off to me, I said, "Thanks, Frannie. Did you know it by heart?"

"Dear me, no, I've got enough useless information clouding my thoughts as it is. I looked Ruth's number up in my little book when you mentioned her name. I'd say to pass my regards on to her, but I've got a feeling Ruth isn't going to be all that happy to hear from you."

"I swear, I won't tell her how I got her number."

Frannie laughed. "You won't have to, she probably already knows."

"What do you mean? How could she?"

"Ruth has always believed she's psychic. If you can make that play to your advantage, it might help your cause. But you need to tiptoe around it. She's sensitive about the subject."

"Thanks, I'll remember that."

After I hung up with Frannie, I took a few deep breaths, then dialed the number she'd given me.

The telephone was answered crisply before it had the chance to complete its first ring.

"Hello?"

"Wow, that was fast," I said.

"I was standing by the phone when it rang," an older woman's voice said. "Would you prefer it if I hung up so you could call me back? I'll let it ring a dozen times before I answer the next time, if you'd like."

"That won't be necessary," I said. She didn't sound all that thrilled with my call in the first place, and I had a hunch if I did as she suggested, she'd never pick up the second time.

"Then I'm glad we've dispensed with that. Now, how may I help you?"

I thought, *You're psychic, don't you already know?* I kept that to myself, though. "My name is Harrison Black. I'm calling about your brother."

"How odd. I've been thinking about him a great deal lately."

"It's imperative that you visit Cyrus as soon as possible. He's living behind two armed guards, and he won't let anyone see him."

"And what is that to you, Mr. Black?"

"Please, call me Harrison. I'm a friend of your brother's, and I'm worried about him."

"He's a grown man, Mr. Black," she said, ignoring my request for informality. I was losing her; I could hear it in her voice. It was time for desperate measures.

"Mrs. Nash, can't you feel his aura from there? I'm afraid your brother is in some kind of trouble. Surely his spirit is calling out to you, his closest relative?"

She paused, then said, "It's obvious you've been talking to Frannie. Don't bother denying it. There was one incident in our childhood, and she's branded me a lunatic ever since. You don't believe in special gifts, do you?"

She had me there, and I couldn't bring myself to lie.

"Honestly, I'm not sure what I think. If you believed in aliens, and for all I know you do, I'd tell you little green men were here if it would help get you to Micah's Ridge to check on your brother."

"What I believe or choose not to believe is none of your business, and I'd appreciate it if you'd drop your references to the psychic world when you speak to me. What exactly is it that you suggest I do, Mr. Black?"

"Visit him," I said. "I'll go with you if you'd like."

"I can't leave here. I have responsibilities to my daughter and her children."

"What about to your brother?" I asked. After the words escaped my mouth, I realized I had probably pushed her too far.

I was nearly ready to apologize when she said, "You're right; of course I'll come. It's going to take me a few days here to arrange for someone to watch the children, but I'll be there as soon as possible, I promise. How do I find you once I'm in town?"

"I'm at the River's Edge complex," I said. "It's next to your land on the Gunpowder River."

"So that's why you're interested in my brother."

"The land development was what made me go see him in the first place, I freely admit that. But I'm worried about Cyrus right now, and it's got nothing to do with what's happening next door to me."

"We'll see if that's true when I get there," she said. "Until then, Mr. Black."

"Good-bye," I said, but she'd already hung up. I wasn't sure how I was going to handle Ruth Nash when she came to town, but the important thing was, if anybody could get through to Cyrus, it would be her. For the moment I was going to have to forget about my friend and hope things were okay until his sister could get there.

I glanced at the clock and realized I'd left Eve alone long enough. It was time to sell candles again.

MARKUM WAS OUTSIDE the candleshop waiting for me when I showed up.

"Have you been waiting long?" I asked. "I didn't realize we were going to meet this afternoon."

"I had some time to kill, so I thought I'd come by. Do you have a minute?"

I looked through the bay window in front of At Wick's End and saw Eve watching us. "I'd really better get inside, but you're welcome to come in."

He shook his head. "No, thanks. That woman doesn't like me, and she's not afraid who knows it."

I wanted to tell him he was being paranoid, but it just so happened he was right. Eve had expressed a dislike for Markum and his way of life since the day I moved into River's Edge. Still, the candleshop was mine to run, and if I wanted Markum there, that was all that counted.

"Come on in," I said. "She won't bite."

"Listen, I don't want to cause any friction between you two. What I've got can wait."

I held the door open. "She needs to accept you, Markum; you're a part of River's Edge."

He walked inside, though it was obvious he was reluctant to do it. Eve stared at us both frostily, as if we'd brought a legion of germs in with us.

"Sorry I took so long," I said. "Markum and I need to talk."

She refused to even acknowledge his presence. "I'm taking my dinner break now if you can spare me."

Since there wasn't a single soul in the candleshop besides the three of us, that didn't look to be a problem. "That's fine," I said.

She grabbed her jacket and was gone in a heartbeat.

Markum grinned after the door closed behind her. "You're right, there's no tension there."

"What exactly does she have against you?" I asked.

"She doesn't approve of my lifestyle."

I put my coat behind the counter and asked, "Why not? I'm surprised she even knows what you do."

Markum laughed. "That's what bugs her so much. She doesn't have a clue how I make my living. All she knows is that I don't make or sell anything, and that I have a lot of free time. The rest is in her imagination."

"So do you think she'd approve if she knew more about your line of work?"

"Are you kidding? She'd probably try to have me evicted."

"She wouldn't have a prayer, not as long as I'm in charge."

"Harrison, you know what I do isn't exactly accepted by the population at large."

"Do you steal things from their rightful owners?" I asked. "Do you cheat the innocent, or rob the rich? In other words, can you stand to look yourself in the mirror when you get up every morning?"

Markum pondered my question for nearly a minute, then said, "I never looked at it that way, but I follow a code of ethics in what I do, though it's nothing that formal. I don't cheat anybody who didn't acquire what they got illegally or immorally, and I'm more interested in restitution than pure profit."

"So we don't have a problem," I said, patting his shoulder.

The big man smiled broadly. "You're good company, you know that? If my Russian deal ever goes through, I'm going to do my best to convince you to come along."

"You never know, I might just take you up on it," I said. "Now what's next?"

He frowned, then said, "I'm not sure. I wanted to discuss some kind of strategy with you before I go muddying up your trail. Have you had any luck on your own?"

I told him about speaking with Runion and his secretary. Markum whistled when he heard the news that Jeanie was going to keep an eye on things for us in the developer's office. "How did you manage that, Harrison? She barely gave me the time of day when I was there."

"I'm not sure," I said, "But I think it had something to do with the way her boss was trying to manipulate me."

"There's got to be more to it than that. What else have you been up to?"

"I got Cyrus's sister to agree to come back to Micah's Ridge. He has two guards patrolling his grounds now. It's the only way I could think to get past them."

"My, you've been busy, haven't you? Anything else I should know about?"

"No, that's about it. Wait a second, there is one more thing." I pulled the excised newspaper clipping out of my wallet and handed it to him. "This is the article Becka cut out of her newspaper."

He studied it a moment, then said, "I wonder why she cut out this article about Hank Klein's donation to the Firefighter's League." I took the clipping back from him and was surprised to see Klein's name mentioned in his own newspaper. I flipped it over and gave it back to him. "I didn't even notice that. How about this woman's body found in Larkspur Lake?"

"We should ask Morton about it."

"I already did," I admitted reluctantly.

"So what did he say?"

"He told me the coroner ruled it an accident, but that's no proof. He thinks Becka killed herself, too, and we know that's not true."

He studied the article a few moments. "Harrison, the circumstances are too different, even though both women died around water. What else do you have?"

I pointed to the snippet about illegal dumping. "I'm willing to admit it could be about this. Don't you think it's too big a coincidence, given the fact that we found an envelope from Washington in her purse and a photo of a barrel in her room?"

"It's a possibility, but coincidences happen in life. What do we really have?"

Suddenly I felt like the dumping was where we should focus and not on the drowning. "The article and the envelope have to be tied together. That picture edge we pulled from her dresser mirror is another piece of it, too."

"Do you think Becka stumbled across something she shouldn't have?"

I nodded. "It's another possibility we have to consider."

"I don't know," Markum said. "For all we know, that letter was something entirely unrelated, and the photograph might have been of her ex-boyfriend, the one she wanted to get rid of."

"So why was the tear left behind?"

"Maybe she got so mad she tore it off the mirror and left that corner by accident. We don't even know it's a barrel; it could be some kind of outdoor chair for all we can tell."

"My gut's telling me we've already got the answer, if we could just find the right way to look at it," I said.

A customer came in and said, "Excuse me, I'm looking for a present for my mother. She's in her early seventies and she's looking for a new hobby."

"You've come to the right place," I told him, then looked at Markum and added, "If you'll hang around a minute, we can talk more about this."

He glanced at his watch, then said, "I need to make some phone calls. We'll discuss it later."

After Markum was gone, I asked the customer what kinds of things his mother liked. "She's a fabulous baker, but she's looking for something else to do with her time." He patted his stomach and said, "If I don't find something else for her to do, she's going to kill me with cookies."

"Does that mean she has a lot of cookie cutters?" I asked.

"You wouldn't believe her collection," he said. "She can't stop buying them. Mother claims the shapes are what she loves."

"Then I've got just the thing for her." I walked over to the aisle with tinted sheet-wax kits and grabbed a few colors. "You should have her try these. She can use her cookie cutters to cut out shapes in the wax. Hang on a second." I'd been experimenting with one-page pamphlets for the store to try to generate some extra business. I grabbed the one I'd written about making specialty candles with cookie cutters and handed him one.

He looked at the brochure, then asked, "What do they look like, though?"

"Let's see what I've got in my classroom." We walked to the back of the store, and after a few minutes of searching the cabinets, I came up with a red honeycombed candle in the shape of a playing-card-club I'd made practicing for a lesson with Mrs. Jorgenson.

He nodded. "This sounds perfect. I'll buy this, too, so I can give Mother an example of what she should be shooting for." He looked embarrassed for a moment when he asked, "It is for sale, isn't it?"

"If you see it here, it's for sale. The only thing we need to haggle over is the price."

As I rang up his purchases, he said, "Can she come by if she's having trouble?"

"I give free advice, but if she's interested, we also teach candlemaking classes here at the store."

"That sounds great," he said. "I'm glad I stopped in."

I handed him his change. "Me, too. Let me know how she likes candlemaking."

"Oh, I will." He took a few steps toward the door, then asked, "Is the owner here today? I'd like to tell her what a good job you're doing."

"I'm the owner myself," I said, "And I appreciate the compliment."

"I complain when the service is bad, so I feel it's my duty to praise where it's merited. Good day."

Goodness help me if I didn't reply, "Good day to

you, sir."

After he was gone, I fielded a few telephone calls, waited on half a dozen of our regular customers and had a generally good time operating my candleshop.

I was running the reports from the register, happy with the afternoon's events, when the front door opened. I'd forgotten to lock it, and a customer right now would throw off my report and cause me an extra half hour of work.

When I saw the look of dogged determination on Erin Lane's face, I was suddenly sorry it wasn't a customer after all.

# Twelve

"THAT look can't be good for me," I said. "What's going on?"

"We're going out on the river," she said.

I felt a wave of dread chill me. "I'm not interested, but thanks for asking."

"Harrison Black, don't you realize the only way you get over being thrown off a horse is to climb right back up on one?"

I pretended to look around. "If you've got a horse, I'm willing to ride it, but I'm not going kayaking again."

"You're being unreasonable, Harrison."

"I think it makes perfect sense," I said. "I'm not getting back in that kayak, and that's final."

"If you won't kayak, how about taking a canoe out with me? It's not the same as paddling alone."

"I'm not sure I'm even willing to do that," I said, remembering the sound of the dull thud on the hull as I'd hit Becka's body.

"If I bring a canoe here, will you go for a ride with me? It doesn't have to be long. I just want you back on the water. Please, Harrison? It's important to me."

"Why?" I asked, sincerely interested in her concern. "Why do you care if I ever paddle again?"

"Because it's my life, and we're getting to be friends. I don't want this to come between us."

I tore the tape off the report and laid it on my till. "Erin, this doesn't have anything to do with you. Can't you understand how I feel?"

"Of course I can. I can't even imagine how horrible the experience must have been for you, but I also know how much you love being out on the water. Come on, Harrison, ten minutes, that's all I'm asking for."

"I don't know," I said, still unsure about how I felt.

"Tell you what, you do this for me, and if you don't enjoy yourself, I'll never ask you to go back on the water again."

I thought about it a few seconds, then said, "Fine, I'll try it. The next time I have some free time, I'll go with you."

She smiled broadly. "I was hoping you'd say that. I have a canoe on the back of my truck. We can be in the water in five minutes."

"Hey, you set me up," I said. I gestured to the report and the till full of money. "I can't leave right now, honest. I have to balance my books, make the deposit and get something to eat. Another time, okay?"

She looked stubborn. "If I let you weasel out of this now, I'll never get you out on the water again. Take your time, do what you need to do, and then we'll go paddling."

"You're not going to give up until I do this, are you?"

She stood firm. "I'm glad you're finally getting the picture."

I shoved the till and the report under the counter. "Then let's get this over with."

"Harrison, it's not a trip to the auditor. We'll have fun, you'll see."

"I'm not making any promises," I said. "Let's go."

She started to say something else, then obviously thought better of it. "That sounds great."

Her truck was in the front lot, and I noticed she'd parked the vehicle as close to the steps that led to the water as she could. As Erin took the bungee-cord fasteners off the canoe, I said, "You really came prepared. What if I'd said no?"

"Then I'd have just had to try again tomorrow, and the next day, and the next."

I laughed despite the fist of dread growing in my gut. "Then I'm glad I said yes. Do you need a hand with that?"

She said, "Sure, that would be great. Grab this end and we'll put it in the water."

After we got the canoe down, she retrieved one of the blue streamlined vests from the front and said, "Put this on."

"Do you actually wear a life preserver yourself? I didn't think you would, after all the time you spent on the water."

"I always wear one, and you should, too. Accidents happen every day." As she strapped hers on, she said, "I never go out without one, and neither should you."

"Okay, I get it." After we had our life jackets on, she handed me a paddle and asked, "Do you mind riding in the front? I'm used to being in back."

"No problem, I'm not bad with the kayak, but a canoe is a completely different kind of boat, isn't it?"

She held her paddle up in the air and said, "It's going to be odd with just one blade, but you'll get used to it. Keep your paddle on the right side of the boat. If we need to correct, I'll do it from where I'm sitting. Are you ready?"

I sighed, then said, "As ready as I'll ever be."

"Come on, this is going to be fun."

"If you say so," I said as I stepped into the boat.

It didn't take long for us to get into a rhythm with our paddling. I'd expected the canoe to be awkward compared to my kayak, but we cut through the water nearly as easily as I did alone. No doubt having an expert like Erin in back helped. I kept scanning the water as we went upstream, searching for anything that might be a body floating around us. There was nothing, though; the water's surface was a flat plane as we cut through it. We hadn't had a drop of rain since Becka's death, and the pristine surface of the water was beautiful. As we paddled on, I started trusting the water again and looked toward the banks around us. The side with River's Edge was soon overgrown and wild, with only the river walk beside the edge to show that we weren't a thousand miles from civilization. As much as I loved Cyrus's walking path, it did spoil the illusion that we were somewhere deep in the wilderness. We paddled in silence, the only noises coming from the movement of our paddles and the birds chirping from their perches near the edge of the Gunpowder.

I was lost in my thoughts when Erin asked, "How are you doing?"

"Better than I expected," I said.

"Are you ready to head back? I promised I wouldn't keep you out long."

I considered going back, and to my surprise, I found that I wasn't ready, at least not yet. "Let's keep going. There's a cove up ahead you've got to see."

I swear I could feel her smiling behind me.


BY THE TIME we got back to River's Edge, I was feeling easy and free on the water again. We pulled the canoe out and carried it to her truck. As Erin secured it, I said, "Thanks, I needed to do that."

"I was glad for the company. We make a good team on the water, Harrison."

"With you in back, I can't imagine you being a part of a bad one."

She shook her head as she secured the last bungee. "Don't kid yourself. I take groups white-water rafting and canoeing, and you'd be amazed how many people want to coast through the rapids when it's the exact time they should be paddling the hardest. I don't know how they get the impression they're on a ride at Disney World. You really should come white water rafting with me sometime."

"Baby steps for now, okay? I'm still going to have to get used to being on the Gunpowder again."

"Maybe we should have gone somewhere else the first time you got back into the water," she said.

"No, this was perfect." I stepped forward and kissed her on the cheek. "Thank you."

She smiled brightly. "You're welcome. Now I've got to get out of here. We stayed out on the water longer than I thought we would, and I've got a group coming by the shop to watch a white-water rafting video."

"Sorry to keep you so long," I said.

"Are you kidding? I had a blast. See you soon, Harrison."

After she was gone, I walked over to the steps that led down to the water and sat. My shoulders were sore from paddling, but it had felt grand being on the water again. It wasn't fair to the Gunpowder to blame the river for what had happened. "Becka," I said softly to myself. "What happened to you?"

"Were you talking to me?" I heard a voice say behind me.

I turned around, and Jeanie, Runion's assistant, was standing there studying me.

"I'm sorry, I didn't know you were there."

She said, "I just got here. The water's really beautiful, isn't it?"

"It's a million-dollar view," I said.

She shuddered. "Don't say that, please."

"Why not?"

Jeanie sat beside me. "It's Runion's favorite expression." She looked out onto the water and added, "You can't put a price tag on this. At least you shouldn't be able to."

"You're right. So, do you have something for me already?"

She shook her head. "No, I haven't had a chance to do any digging. I was just curious about your setup out here, so I thought I'd stop by." She glanced back at the darkened stores and said, "I'm too late, aren't I?"

"It's never too late for a tour of the candleshop," I said. "Come on in."

"Are you sure it's not a problem?" she asked. "I don't want to keep you from anything."

"My schedule's all clear," I said.

She enjoyed her tour of the shop, and I persuaded her to take a pack of wax sheets. "Let me pay for this," she said.

I pointed to one corner of the sheet. "The honeycomb is crushed here, do you see? You can trim it and make a perfectly good candle, the directions are printed on the back, but I won't sell it if it's damaged."

"You really care about this place, don't you?" she asked.

"It's not just my job; it's become my life."

"I envy you that," she said as I walked her out of the shop and to her car.

"Thanks for the tour," she said.

"I'm glad you came by."

To my surprise, she leaned forward, as if she was expecting me to kiss her. I wasn't sure what to do next, but I was saved by a call from the deck of the complex. "Harrison, do you have a moment?"

"I'll be right there, Pearly."

Jeanie started to kiss my cheek, then paused and settled for a handshake instead. "Thanks again."

"Come back any time," I said.

"Even if I don't have anything to report?" she asked.

"My door's always open for you, Jeanie. I love sharing what I know about making candles."

She studied me a second, then asked, "You're not like most guys, are you?"

I laughed. "It depends. Is that a good thing in your eyes or not?"

She smiled. "Oh, it's a good thing, you can believe

that. We were alone together for half an hour and you never made a single pass at me."

"I don't know you that well yet," I said, surprised by her candor, and mine in reply.

"Believe me, that's usually not an issue. Good night, Harrison."

"Good night, Jeanie."

I waited until she drove off, then joined Pearly in front of The Crocked Pot. He was sitting in one of Millie's café chairs, and I pulled another one from under the awning and joined him.

Pearly said, "I didn't mean to interrupt."

"You didn't," I said. "I wasn't expecting Jeanie to come by."

"I saw the way she was looking at you. She'll be back, and soon." He paused, then added, "And I'm willing to wager you'll be glad when she does."

"Forgive me, but I'm not in the mood to be analyzed this evening," I said.

He looked as if I'd slapped him. "I'm the one who should be asking for forgiveness. Sometimes I forget myself."

"Pearly, I didn't mean anything by it. It's just been a long day."

"For me as well," he said.

"So what's on your mind?"

"I've spoken with both Sanora and Heather, and I'm afraid I need some advice before I decide how best to proceed."

"You want advice from me?" I asked. "If we're down to that, I'm afraid it's pretty hopeless."

He shook his head. "Don't be so certain of that,

Harrison. It appears that the main source of contention between them is you."

"Me? You can't be serious," I said. "How could I be the problem?"

"Oh, I'm not even certain they're aware of it. They both claim it's a territorial issue, but I feel you're at the heart of their conflict."

"I've never dated either one of them," I said. "Are you telling me they both have crushes on me?"

Pearly let a slight smile slip out before he reined it in. "Nothing that dramatic, I'm afraid," he said. "They aren't fighting over your affection, but rather your friendship. In my conversations with both women, the recurring underlying theme was how much time you spend with the other woman. The currents of discord are rather strong."

"So what do I do about it? I barely have time enough to handle everything as it is, let alone add extra visits to each of them."

"We make time for the things that are important to us, Harrison. If you want both women to stay, I'm afraid it's up to you."

"Of course I want them to stay," I said. "But I can't do anything as overt as coming right out and telling them."

"I'm afraid that's exactly what you're going to have to do, or both women will leave."

"How sure are you?" I asked. It was hard to believe that the dispute between Sanora and Heather was as simple as Pearly was making it out to be.

"I'm as certain as I can be, given the circumstances. Talk to them, Harrison. Make them feel needed and wanted here."

"And if it doesn't work?" I asked.

"Then I'm afraid you're going to have to find two new tenants."

I stood and stretched. "I'll do my best," I said. "Thanks for looking into this, Pearly."

"It was more rewarding than I expected," he said. "Perhaps I was premature in my decision to retire."

Oh, no. Was I going to lose Pearly, too? "I don't know how I can run this place without you, but I want you to do whatever makes you happy."

"Thank you, my friend. Good night."

I said good night as well and headed upstairs. I was on the third step when I remembered the cash till and report I'd shoved under the counter to go canoeing with Erin. Letting out a loud sigh, I turned and headed back to At Wick's End. If I was lucky, the report would balance and I could get the deposit to the bank before I nodded off and crashed my truck.

The balance was off by five dollars, not a horrible deficit, but one that would bother me the rest of the night. I'd just about resigned myself to losing the money when I started to put the till back into the cash register and found that an errant bill had slipped under the drawer somehow. Relieved with the corrected balance, I made out the deposit, but found I was too tired from the day's events to risk driving to the bank. I tucked the deposit bag under my arm, promised myself I'd take care of it early the next morning, then went upstairs and straight to bed. The emotional time I'd been going through lately was finally catching up with me, and all I really wanted was to go to my place and forget the outside world even existed.

# Thirteen

WHEN I woke up the next morning, it was spitting rain outside my window and thunder boomed in the distance. From the look of the sky, we were in for more before the storm system was through with us. At least I wouldn't have to go back on the river anytime soon. I'd enjoyed my time with Erin on the water, but I wasn't in any real hurry to repeat it. Maybe some day I'd take the kayak out again on my own, but I wasn't ready, despite the success of yesterday's excursion. I didn't doubt Erin would have knocked on my door first thing if it hadn't been storming out. I'd take the reprieve where I could get it.

I opened my door and found my copy of the *Gunpowder Gazette* on my stoop. It cost me a little extra to have it delivered upstairs, but I was willing to pay for it, since it meant that if the young man delivering didn't do it, I'd have to climb down the steps and back up again in my robe.

I opened the paper as I walked back inside my apartment and suddenly lost my appetite. There was a front page article about Greg Runion, accompanied by a photo of him with his largest grin glued firmly in place. I scanned the article to see that the *Gazette* was backing Runion's development plans, and I wondered how much the endorsement had cost the developer. I hoped it was a fortune.

I got dressed quickly without having the stomach to finish the article, let alone the rest of the paper, and headed down to Millie's for a quick cup of coffee and one of her baked ambrosia treats. The place was half-full with a smattering of customers, but no one even looked up from their papers or their meals as I came in.

"Morning," I said as I reached for the coffee she had ready and waiting for me the second I'd walked in.

"Good morning, Harrison. It's a lovely day, isn't it?"

I looked back outside for a second, wondering if the sun had broken through the clouds when I hadn't been paying attention. No, it was still cool and wet and gray outside. "You like this weather?"

She laughed. "Harrison Black, if I wanted sunshine every day, I'd move to Southern California. I like having lots of rowdy weather. It makes me feel alive."

"So why don't you move to New England?" I asked. "They get lots of interesting weather up there."

She huffed once. "I see you're in a mood today, aren't you? What's brought that on?"

"Have you read the paper today?"

She frowned. "Are you talking about that Runion man's advertisement that doubled as a story? It's shameful, isn't it?"

"I think so. He's not going to be happy until all of

Micah's Ridge is paved over, but I was beginning to think I was the only one upset about it."

I hadn't noticed Sanora sitting in back. She piped up, "Harrison, that's a rather narrow way of looking at things, isn't it? Not all development is bad."

"Sanora, don't tell me you support him."

She sipped her coffee, then said, "I like to make my decisions on a case-by-case basis. If a developer hadn't come in here and erected this building, we'd all be working in huts. I, for one, cherish a roof over my head."

"That's not what I meant," I said.

She stood and drained her coffee. As she walked to the door, she said, "So as long as the expansion stops after you've got your place, you're a happy man."

Before I could think of anything to say in rebuttal, she was gone.

Millie smiled gently. "You know what? She's got a point."

"Don't you turn on me, too," I said. "Any chance you have one of your glorious treats for me this morning? I'm in dire need of your baking."

"I'm sorry, Harrison, I don't have a single thing for you today."

She noticed the shocked expression on my face, then added quickly, "I'm teasing you, Harrison. You know I always hold something just for you."

She disappeared in back and came out a minute later holding a platter covered with a gingham dish cloth. "I think you might like one of these. I don't ordinarily make them this time of year, but I thought you could use a special little pick-me-up."

I could smell the heavenly aroma before she even

unveiled the plate. "Pumpkin doughnuts," I said as I took the offered goodies from her.

"They're all just for you. I made one batch, and every one of them has your name on it, if you're interested. I love to bake when it's raining, and I know how you love these."

"I feel like I just won the lottery," I said as I inhaled the heavenly aroma.

A man from one of the back tables joined us and said, "Sorry, I didn't mean to eavesdrop. Okay, that's a lie. The second I smelled those doughnuts, I knew I had to have one. How much are they?"

"I'm sorry," Millie said, "but these aren't for sale. They're a gift. If you come back in October, I make them through Christmas Eve."

He looked so sad that I broke down and handed him one from the pile. I'd just have to find a way to live with eleven. "Here, have one on me. I've got to warn you, though, they're addicting."

He took a bite, then another, and as we stood there, he polished the whole doughnut off.

"Ma'am, that was the best thing I've ever eaten in my life. I want to place a standing order with you, a dozen of those beauties every Monday morning. I don't think I'd be able to get through the week without them now that I've tried one."

"Sorry, but the smallest special-order batch I make is six dozen. As I said, I'll be glad to sell you all you want come October."

I knew Millie made smaller quantities than seventy-two—I was holding one at the moment—but I kept that fact to myself. I wasn't about to do anything to get myself out of her good graces.

He was unfazed by her extravagant demand though. "Six dozen it is." He reached into his wallet and pulled out a hundred-dollar bill and a business card. "Let me know when that runs out and I'll replace it. You can call me next Monday to let me know when I can pick up the first batch."

Millie didn't know what to think, but she took the man's money, and he was soon gone. She looked at me and said, "Harrison, I had no intention of making these for sale again this time of year."

"You've got a reason to now," I said. "Any chance you could make a few dozen every Monday and slip some under my pillow?"

She swatted me lightly with the towel in her hands. "You're as bad as he is. Don't you have a business to run?"

I nodded. "As soon as I get a pint of milk, I'll be out of your hair."

She retrieved one from the cooler, and I said, "Thanks again, these are wonderful." As I walked out, I heard her muttering to herself, "I can't believe that man took me up on it. What's the world coming to?"

I walked down to At Wick's End and unlocked the front door. I had the best breakfast a man could ask for, and the solitude of my candleshop to enjoy them in a leisurely fashion.

Life was looking up indeed.

I ate three doughnuts, though I'd promised myself to stop at two. If I didn't start kayaking again, and soon, I was going to have to start walking for exercise again. Being in such close proximity to Millie was definitely a detriment to my waistline.

Eve came in twenty minutes before it was time to open, and I was glad I'd finished eating before she showed up. Though it was my candleshop, I still felt like a child in school around her sometimes.

She sniffed the air, then said, "Harrison, have you been experimenting with scents again?"

"I call it Pumpkin Surprise," I said. "Do you like it?"

"It's a tad strong, isn't it?" Eve wasn't a big fan of jocularity. It was time to come clean.

"Actually, Millie made me a special order of pumpkin doughnuts. Would you like one?"

She shook her head. "I've had my breakfast, thank you very much."

"I'm sure it was sensible and well-balanced," I said softly, but not softly enough.

"Some of us have to watch our figures," she said icily and disappeared back in the storeroom. "I'll be doing our inventory. Surely you can handle our customers until I'm finished." My last crack was going to cost me, but I didn't care. It was amazing just how much better I felt after eating my favorite comfort food.

I opened the front door on the dot of nine and was startled to find Mrs. Jorgenson standing in front of the shop. As I let her in, I offered to take her coat, which was soaking wet. "Did we have a lesson planned for today?" I asked.

She shook her head. "No, but I'm in need of more supplies. I trust you can assist me."

"Yes, ma'am, I'm at your service." As I followed her to the waxes, dyes and scents, I added, "Have you gone through your first batch already?"

She sniffed the air. "Let's just say I'm still unsatisfied with my results so far."

"What seems to be the problem?" I asked. "Maybe I can help."

She frowned, then said, "Harrison, you know how I feel about soliciting free advice."

I suddenly thought about what a resource for Micah's Ridge I had before me. "Tell you what; I'll swap you for information. I'll answer your questions about candle-making, and you answer mine about who really runs Micah's Ridge."

It was taking a chance, approaching her like that, and if I'd had more time to think about it, I probably would have chickened out. After all, Mrs. Jorgenson and her extravagant forays into the candlemaking world were becoming a necessity to my bottom line.

She thought about it a full minute, then said, "You know I don't believe in gossip, don't you?"

"Yes, ma'am, and I would never ask you anything about anyone that was of a personal nature. I'm more concerned about who says jump and who says how high."

She nodded. "I can agree to that then, at least on principle. What would you like to know?"

I said, "You first. What are the candles doing?"

She looked down at her hands and said, "Actually, I'm having a difficult time getting them out of their molds."

"Did you use the release I sold you?"

She said, "I used some, but the directions made me quite cautious against overusing it. I do hate chemicals."

I said patiently, "Don't be afraid to coat the interior. If you don't like the spray, you can add stearin to your wax. That works like a charm. Don't use it in rubber molds though; it eats right through them over time."

She said, "That sounds simple enough." She grabbed a few blocks of wax from the shelves, some stearin, a selection of scents and dyes, then she asked, "What would you like to know?"

"What do you know about Greg Runion?"

She bristled slightly at the question. "Harrison, I told you I'm not a gossip."

"I don't care if he wears pink ruffles at home or dances with pigs. I want to know if he's got the resources to pull off this major development he's planning."

Mrs. Jorgenson frowned. "Yes, I saw that disgraceful story in the paper this morning as well. Might I ask why you're suddenly so interested in Greg Runion?"

"A friend of mine has been taken in by the man, and I'm concerned about him."

"As well you should be," she said gently. "You asked if he has the resources to finance his latest scheme. My guess would be no."

"So where's he getting his backing? Is he using Cyrus Walters's money?"

"Do you know Cyrus?" Mrs. Jorgenson asked.

"Yes, we've become friends. At least I thought so."

"Now that's a curious comment. Why do you say that?"

"He threw me out of his house a few days ago, and when I came back to straighten things out, there was a guard posted at the front door."

Mrs. Jorgenson frowned, stared out the bay window in front of the shop, then said, "Harrison, you must never tell her I suggested this, but there's only one thing to do. You must call his sister in West Virginia."

"Thanks, but I already spoke with Ruth, and she's coming as soon as she can get away."

Mrs. Jorgenson eyed me carefully. "Why, Harrison,

you've become quite resourceful, haven't you? Ruth will cut through this nonsense, you can rest assured on that point."

"So what should I know about Greg Runion?"

"I've heard rumors that he has a financial backer on this project of his to turn the banks of the Gunpowder River into a nightmare of condominiums."

"Who is it?" I asked.

"I'm sure you don't know the gentleman, but perhaps I could arrange an introduction, if I handle it just so."

"Thanks, I'd really appreciate that," I said. "So, are you going to tell me his name, or is it shrouded in mystery?"

"It won't mean anything to you, but I'll tell you if you promise you'll keep it to yourself."

"I promise," I said, wondering who this financial backer was.

"Grover Blake," she said in a hushed voice.

"I've met him," I said. "In fact, I just had some of his barbecue."

Mrs. Jorgenson sniffed the air. "Honestly, I don't know why you bother asking me things. You seem to know everything going on in Micah's Ridge."

I tried to mollify her. Mrs. Jorgenson was one person in town I couldn't afford to alienate. I said, "I was under the impression that Grover gave all of his money away when he moved back here."

She smiled at that. "Then you don't know everything. It makes a quaint story, but that's all it is. He's got more assets than I do, and that's saying something for our part of North Carolina. So what are you going to do with this information?"

"I'm going to go talk to him."

"Be careful, Harrison. All is not as it seems there."

I thanked her, then said, "Tell you what, you've paid for your purchase today with information. This is all on the house."

"Nonsense, I pay my way and you know it. Ring these up so I can get started on my next pour."

I did as I was told and totaled the supplies as she added more items to her pile. Eve poked her head out of the storeroom. "I thought I heard voices," she said, her words fading as she saw who my customer was.

"I'm going to walk Mrs. Jorgenson out," I said, "then I've got an errand to run."

"Of course," Eve said. "Nice to see you again, ma'am."

"I'm sure," Mrs. Jorgenson said in reply. She wasn't big on mingling with anyone but the owner of the store, but I had to give Eve credit. She never gave up trying to engage the woman.

I walked Mrs. Jorgenson out to her car. As she got in, she said, "Remember, Harrison, there are more layers to this than you might realize. Watch your step."

"Surely you don't think Grover's a threat, do you?"

She pursed her lips. "If he takes it in his mind not to like you, you'll live to regret it, I promise you that. I've seen it happen too many times before. Remember, he might sound like a sweet old man, but Grover is as sharp as a razor."

I said good-bye, then jumped in the Ford truck and headed over to Grover's barbecue stand and backyard. I had another reason to watch my step. It would be bad enough to be banished from ever coming back to

Grover's and miss that succulent barbecue, but if I got Markum blackballed, I wasn't sure he'd ever be able to forgive me.

And I wouldn't even be able to find it in my heart to blame him.

# Fourteen

I found Grover watching over the fire in his backyard pit. There were no cars parked by the road when I pulled the truck in, so I'd have his full attention.

"Good morning," I said as I approached.

"Harrison Black," he said neutrally. "The sign's not out, or didn't Markum tell you what to look for?"

"Actually he didn't."

"There's an old red shirt I hang from a tree branch when I'm serving," he said. "Other times I like to be left alone."

There was no mistaking the tone in his voice, that this was one of those other times, but there was no way I was going to wait to approach him about Runion with half of the power structure of Micah's Ridge looking on.

"I need to talk to you about something, Grover. Believe me, I wouldn't bother you if it wasn't important."

He poked a thick slab of wood under the cooker and

watched the smoke a moment. "Most folks don't like to press me," he said quietly.

There was a distinct chill in his voice now.

"I'm worried about what Greg Runion is going to do to Micah's Ridge."

Grover's gaze snapped from the fire to me. "What's that got to do with me?"

"I know you're backing him," I said softly.

Grover tried to bring off a fake laugh, but he'd hesitated too long before deciding on his course of action. "Man, haven't you heard? I gave all my money away when I came back home. Why else would I sell my barbecue from a place like this?"

"Look, I'm not here to refute the legend you've built up for yourself, and the last thing I want to do is anything that's going to keep me from your barbecue, but you can't let him do this. Do you have any idea what the river's going to look like? He's going to destroy it."

"It's no business of mine," Grover said abruptly.

"I wish I could believe that," I said.

The fire under the cooker was now completely forgotten. "Mr. Black, I'll ask you to leave now."

"You can't let him do this," I said.

"I said go!" He was as furious with me as I was with him. "You're not welcome here anymore."

I gave up. There was no way I was going to be able to break through his resolve. "Fine, let it happen, then. It's on your head, not mine."

I was five steps away when he called out to me, "Mr. Black, hold up a second."

Had he changed his mind? I turned and saw that look in his eyes, the look of anger and just a little hate for me. "You can tell Markum he's not welcome here, either."

I lost my temper. "That's just plain mean, Grover. He had nothing to do with me being here. Banish me if you want to, but don't take it out on him."

Grover spat on the ground, then turned his back on me and gave his full attention back to the fire.

I had no choice. I'd come looking for answers, but instead all I'd managed to do was to bring my friend grief.

How in the world was I going to tell Markum what I'd done?

THERE WAS NOTHING else I could do but look for my friend and give him the bad news. What if he showed up at Grover's as soon as that T-shirt went up? I couldn't stand the thought of him going through a shunning with everyone looking on. I drove back to River's Edge and went upstairs to his office, hoping that he'd be in his office.

He was, and I suddenly found myself wishing that I'd been able to delay conveying the news a while, say a year or two.

Markum was deep in thought studying a geological survey map when I walked in. He had it spread out over his desk, and he looked up as I entered. "Harrison, you should see this. I might have found something."

As much as I could have used the distraction, I knew I had to tell him the bad news before I lost my nerve. "I've got something I have to tell you," I said solemnly.

The map was quickly forgotten. "What is it? Has something happened?"

"I messed up, and I'm sorry. I don't think I was wrong to do it, but I should have talked to you first."

Markum leaned back in his chair and ran a hand through the tangle of his thick black hair. "Is it something we can fix?"

"I'm afraid not," I said.

"Well, don't just sit there, tell me what you've done."

I took a deep breath, then admitted, "I just talked to Grover. I confronted him, if you want to know the truth, and he banned me from his place. You, too," I added, not able to meet his gaze.

There was too much silence for too long, so I forced myself to look up. Markum had his fingers intertwined, and he was studying them carefully. After what seemed like a lifetime, he said, "Maybe you'd better tell me about it."

"I didn't go there looking for trouble, I swear it. Mrs. Jorgenson told me Grover was backing Runion's bid to take over the river bank."

"He's broke," Markum snapped. "I doubt he's got two dimes to rub together."

"That's the story he likes to tell, isn't it? Mrs. Jorgenson told me she's one of the few folks in Micah's Ridge who knows the truth. Markum, he never gave any of his money away. Grover's been feeding that to folks right along with his barbecue."

"So naturally you felt the need to call him on it," Markum said.

"Doesn't anybody around here care that they're going to destroy the land around us with condos?"

"And ruin your view in the process."

I stood up. "Listen, I understand that you're mad, but this isn't just about me."

"Harrison, if they were doing this in Hickory or Bethlehem on the Catawba, would you be so upset?"

I paused, then said, "I'd like to think so. Listen, I'm sorry this happened."

"So am I," he said.

"So is that it? Did I just kill our friendship?"

He studied me for a few moments, then said, "Not over barbecue, no matter how good it is. I just wish you'd talked to me first. Maybe we could have found a way to look into it without this happening."

"I'm sorry," I repeated.

"Don't worry about it. So what do we do now?"

"I'm going to forget about Runion until Cyrus's sister Ruth gets here. Until then, I'm going to dig into Becka's death more."

"And sell a candle or two along the way, too, right?"

"I'm always up for that."

I left him at his desk, sorry that I'd cost him something so dear. It was a casualty of my nosiness that I shouldn't have taken a chance with. Markum had suffered from my mistake, and I was determined to make it up to him. Maybe I'd go on his next salvage and recovery job after all; he'd asked me enough in the time since we'd met. If I made it back in one piece, the grand gesture would be worth it. He was right about one thing. Friendship was more important than good barbecue, though there were folks in the South who would stone me if I said it aloud.

ON MY WAY downstairs to the candleshop, I decided to pop in on Heather and try to put Pearly's advice to work. It was hard to believe that I held the key to her staying. I just hoped I didn't botch the job.

She was in the middle of selling a vast array of

crystals and amethysts to an elderly man when I walked into The New Age, so I nodded to her, then browsed among the trays of polished stones. There was a great variety there, and I felt myself drawn to pick up one sample stone of each, hold it in my hand, then move on to the next selection.

I didn't even notice the man was gone until Heather coughed gently. I dropped the adventurine in my hand and let it slip back to the pile.

"They're lovely, aren't they?" she said. "Most of these stones came from Hiddenite." Hiddenite was a place an hour's drive from Micah's Ridge, and they had unbelievable deposits of precious and semiprecious stones there.

"I thought you just got your quartz there," I said.

"I do, but these are locally mined, too. You've got the touch for stones, don't you?"

"What do you mean?" I asked.

"I saw the way you were bonding with them," she said.

"I was just looking," I insisted.

She smiled gently. "So which stone attracted you the most?"

"I liked this one," I admitted, pointing to a translucent parallelogram I'd picked up and studied earlier. It hadn't been in a bin, but instead stood on a piece of black velvet. "Was this quartz polished into its shape at all?"

"No, it crystallizes naturally that way." She picked the stone up and added, "It's Calcite, actually, and it's one of the few pieces in my shop that didn't come from the United States." She gave it to me, and I felt the stone's weight in my hand again.

"So what does that say about me?" I asked, trying to ease her sincerity. I didn't put much stock in rocks, crystals, pyramids or many of the other things Heather sold in her shop.

If she caught my jibe she didn't acknowledge it. "You're a man who loves order. You'd like things in the world to be more defined than they are, but you also have a skewed sense of value compared to most people. You're not concerned with acquiring great wealth, but you would like to acquire more friends than you've got. I wouldn't say you're a risk-taker, but you are willing to go out pretty far out on a limb when someone you care about is involved."

I put the stone back on the velvet. "How much of that did you get from the stone, and how much from knowing me?"

She smiled again. "Perhaps I fudged a little, but I have found it's true that our preferences reveal more about our natures than most people realize."

"Heather, I really need you to stay at River's Edge. I'd miss you too much if you were gone."

"Me, or Esmeralda?" Now she was the one trying to lighten the mood, but I wasn't going to let her.

"You," I said earnestly. "I really want you to stay here with us."

"Then don't renew Sanora's lease," she said.

"I want you both here," I said.

"But she—"

I cut her off. "Don't do this."

She frowned, then a customer walked in before I could push her for a commitment.

"Excuse me," she said.

"We're not finished."

"It can wait," Heather said. Her customer was wearing a simple designer dress that must have cost her a fortune. From the way she was draped in stones, it appeared that she had an affinity for diamonds.

I slipped out as Heather waited on her customer. Instead of going back to the candleshop, I decided to speak with Sanora first. Maybe I'd have better luck with her.

Unfortunately, she was taking the day off, or so the sign in the window of The Pot Shot said. I wished I knew how she could afford to be gone so much from her store. Whatever her secret was, I doubted it was anything I could apply to At Wick's End. I'd tried several ways to bring in new customers, but I'd had tepid results from my marketing plans. We were getting by, though, and that was going to have to be good enough for now. Once I figured out what had really happened to Becka, maybe I could focus more on the business, but until I knew the truth, the candles would have to wait.

I popped in to tell Eve I was going to be gone longer than I expected and was surprised to see half a dozen customers in the shop.

She looked relieved, almost happy to see me when we made eye contact. In a loud voice, she said, "The proprietor just walked in. I'm sure he'll be glad to answer your questions."

So much for my plans. I plastered the most sincere smile I could manage onto my face and said, "How may I help you?"

A middle-aged woman with blonde streaks through her auburn hair said, "I'm not having any success at all with my marbling. Can you tell me what I'm doing wrong?"

I'd studied the technique of putting powdered dustings of different dyes onto a candle, then melting them with a hand torch, but I'd never tried it myself. "Tell me what's happening and I'll see if I can help."

"Just when I start getting some good color flow, the candles keep melting on me."

"Try hitting the candle with brief bursts of heat instead of a steady blast."

"But the dyes won't incorporate that way."

"Be patient and it will work fine," I said, hoping the author of the candlemaking book I'd read had done more research than I had.

I must have convinced her, because she bought another selection of powdered dyes and a large pack of dipped candles I'd made myself. As I wrapped the candles individually in white paper, I said, "If you have any more trouble, come back and I'd be glad to help you." I'd make it a point to practice the technique myself before she returned. After all, I enjoyed the varied ways there were to make and embellish candles.

"Thank you so much," she said.

"Who's next?" I asked.

A young man who couldn't be more than fifteen approached when no one else did and said, "I'm looking for something, I don't know, kind of cool and easy to do, too."

I led him to the sheets of wax we sold for rolling candles, one of the easiest ways there was to make candles. "These are fun," I said.

"It's for my girlfriend's birthday," he admitted.

"What's her favorite color?"

"She's nuts about purple."

I showed him two different shades we carried, and he said, "Which one should I get?"

"Why not both?" I suggested. "That way she can make a taper with two shades in it."

"Is it tough to do?" he asked, studying the back of one of the packages.

"No, they're pretty easy if she follows the directions."

He studied the price, then said, "I guess I'll just take one."

I nodded, then said, "You know what? I forgot to put a sign up. We're having a special, buy one pack and get one free." I didn't have the heart to turn him down.

"Really?" He brightened. "That would be great."

Unfortunately, one of the women shopping overheard me. She called to two of her friends. "Did you hear that, girls? We've found our Christmas presents for our grandkids."

Great. I was never going to hear the end of if from Eve. We'd make enough to cover our costs, but I'd managed to lose a good chunk of profit. Maybe there was a way I could salvage something. "Limit one per customer," I said loudly.

"So we'll each buy one," the woman said. "There's lot of other stuff here."

After everyone was gone, Eve said, "I wasn't aware that we were having a sale."

"I was just helping the poor kid out," I admitted.

Instead of the reproach I'd been expecting, Eve smiled. "Harrison, there are more important things than the bottom line. Who knows? You may have created a new candlemaker today."

I smiled. "There are worse things I could do, aren't there?"

"The next time, though, you might want to keep your voice down when you're offering unadvertised specials."

"Yeah, that's something to keep in mind."

The rest of the day was fairly quiet, though we managed to make several more sales. As dusk approached, the shop was closed, the books balanced, and I was on my way to the bank so I could get the deposit in.

As I drove through Micah's Ridge, I saw a man coming out of a building on King Street. I didn't need a second look to know that it was one of the men Markum and I had seen coming out of Becka's apartment the day we broke in.

# Fifteen

I pulled the truck over into a parking spot and waited for him to catch up with me on foot. It was one of the few times in my life that I wished I had a cell phone. Who would I call, though? Sheriff Morton probably wouldn't believe me. I knew I could trust Markum, and though we'd had some disagreements lately, I still wanted him at my back. It would have felt good having anybody in the cab of the truck with me at the moment, including my feline friend Esmeralda.

I slumped down in the driver's seat as the man approached and found myself praying he wouldn't look my way. He didn't pay the Ford the slightest attention as he walked past. The man was intent on something, mostly unaware of the world around him.

I waited until he was a block past me, then I slipped out of my truck and started following him on foot. I'd locked the deposit up in the glove box, so at least there wouldn't be a repeat of what had happened to me once before. I couldn't bear the thought of losing another deposit because of my own carelessness. There were several groups of strollers out walking the streets of Micah's Ridge, though all the stores but Hannalee's Icy Treats were closed. Hannalee made the ice creams she sold herself, using the highest butterfat she could from a dairy herd just out of town. It was good enough so that folks came from Hickory, Lenoir, Elkton Falls, Harper's Landing, Bethlehem and Boone for a taste of one of her special blends.

I thought the stranger was going to duck into Hannalee's for a second, but he passed it by. I followed him, being careful not to be spotted, though it didn't appear the man would notice me if I were on fire. He turned down a side street, and I hurried after him so I wouldn't lose him.

As I turned the corner, I felt myself being flung back against the side of the brick building. The man I'd been following had me pinned against the wall with a broken piece of wood he must have found nearby. The board was jammed into my chest, making it hard to breathe and nearly impossible to move. It appeared that I hadn't been nearly as slick as I thought I had following him.

He said in a low voice, "Okay, what do you want?"

"What are you talking about?" I sputtered.

"You've been tailing me for three blocks. What do you think, I'm blind? I asked you a question."

He pressed harder on my chest, and I felt my lungs constrict from the pressure of the wood.

"You know what I want," I said. "What happened to Becka Lane?"

That got his attention, but not in a good way. He was really applying the pressure now. "What about her? Who are you?"

"What did you do to her?"

He looked at me a second, then said, "Buddy, you've got the wrong guy. I never laid a hand on her."

"You're lying. I saw you coming out of her apartment. I wasn't alone, either."

He shook his head. "I was doing a favor for a friend. I don't guess it's going to do any good telling you I didn't touch her."

"No good at all," I said. "Who's the friend you're doing a favor for?"

"That, you'll never know. Listen, this is going to hurt a little, but it shouldn't kill you."

He eased the pressure on my chest when he removed the board, but I didn't like the way he was shifting it in his grip. It looked like he had every intention of clobbering me.

I was painfully aware that I was on my own, but there was no reason to let him know that. I looked back toward the main road and shouted, "Come on out. He's not going to tell me."

He looked around to see who I was talking to. I did the only thing I could think of to save myself. I stomped on his foot the second he shifted his attention from me. To my surprise, it actually worked. He dropped his weapon and crouched down in pain. I started to run, then I realized I still hadn't gotten the information I was after. I picked up the wood, took the jagged edge and shoved it into his neck. The way he knelt down, he had no choice but to take it. A few dots of blood welled up, and he said, "Cut that out."

"Tell me who you were doing a favor for," I said.

"Get that wood off my neck or I'm not telling you a thing."

I pushed it harder against him, and he grunted in pain. The only thing sustaining me was remembering how it had felt hitting Becka's body with my kayak. "If you don't talk, I'll use more than the end of this board on you."

Maybe there was something in my voice, or maybe he didn't owe that many favors, because he said, "Okay, I'll tell you. It's not that big a deal."

"I'm waiting," I said.

"Hank Klein had us check out this chick's apartment. We didn't even know who she was."

"You're talking about the newspaper publisher? Why should I believe you?"

"He was dating her. We went there to look for a letter the fool had written, but we couldn't find it. Somebody called the cops on us."

"Why would you do a favor for Klein?"

The man grunted. "We both owed him one. Now you want to let up on that thing? My neck's killing me."

"How do I know you won't come after me if I let you go."

"You'll still have the board, won't you? Listen, I've been pretty reasonable about this up to now, but if this doesn't end right now, it's going to be personal. Do you get me?"

I took the pressure off him and said, "Go ahead. Get up."

He did, eyeing me as he rubbed his neck. "Man, you've got a mean streak I wasn't counting on, and I'm usually pretty good at judging people."

"Like you said, it's different when it's personal. Don't try to find me, you understand?"

He laughed. "You've been watching too much television. I figure we're square, at least for now."

I watched him walk away, thought about following him to see who he was going to meet, then I realized he'd probably lose me before I got half a block.

I was still carrying the wood in my hand when I came back onto the main street, so I dropped it against the edge of the building and walked back to my truck. Thankfully none of the windows were shattered, and the money was right where I'd left it, locked safely in the glove box.

I drove to the bank, dropped off my deposit, then decided to pay a visit to the newspaper publisher. Maybe if I caught him off guard while he was at home, I might be able to get something out of him.

I looked up the address in the telephone book, found Klein's place and drove there. After two sessions with the doorbell of the Colonial, Wanda Klein answered. She'd accused me of murder once, something that naturally still left a bad taste in my mouth.

"What do you want?" she snarled at me.

"I need to see your husband."

"He doesn't have time for the likes of you," she said. "Go home."

From the other room, I heard the publisher's voice. "Wanda? Who is it? The phone's for you."

She was clearly torn between chastising me more and seeing who was calling her. She made her decision, slamming the door in my face without another word. I waited ten seconds, then I rang the bell again. I was nothing if not persistent.

Hank Klein came out. "Go away," he said.

"I'm not done talking to your wife. I'm sure she'd love to know about your girlfriend."

He shot a glance back inside, then stepped out on the

porch and pulled the door shut behind him. "Keep your voice down, you moron."

"I don't have anything to hide," I said. "Don't tell me your wife doesn't know you were dating Becka."

"Who fed you that nonsense? We weren't dating."

"That's a lie. You were seen out on a date with Becka right before she died. It was a public place, Klein."

"The pizza joint?" he asked. "You've got to be kidding me. She didn't like an editorial I wrote, and if you knew anything at all about the woman, Becka wasn't shy about sharing her opinions with the world."

He had a point; she never ducked confrontation, but I wasn't ready to give in that easily. "Maybe that's true, but I've got another witness, one of your own associates."

"What, somebody at the paper told you I was dating Becka Lane? That's a load of crap, I've never cheated on my wife in my life. I don't dare take the chance."

"What are you talking about?"

"Not that it's any of your business, but the newspaper belongs to her father. I'm the editor by her capricious whim. Newspapering is the only thing I know. Do you think I'm foolish enough to risk losing it? Who is this associate you're talking about? I'm firing whoever it was first thing in the morning."

"I don't know his name, but he said you asked him to break into Becka's apartment right after she was murdered."

He shook his head. "Harrison, I don't know why you should believe me, but he lied to you."

Could he be telling me the truth? I considered myself a pretty good judge of character. If Klein was lying to me, he was doing it pretty convincingly.

"So what are you going to do," he said, "ruin my

marriage and my career based on what some thug told you?"

"No, I don't work that way," I said. "But let me warn you, if you had anything to do with Becka's death, I'll make sure you're punished for it."

Klein rubbed his chin. "Morton told me it was a suicide. What makes you think he was wrong?"

"Becka hated pills," I said. "She didn't exactly keep it a secret, either."

"So let me get this straight. You think I was her boyfriend, and that I killed her to cover up our affair. Harrison, think about it. If we were dating, wouldn't I know she hated pills? I would have come up with some other way of getting rid of her if I'd known that. If she didn't kill herself, you need to think about who wanted her dead and didn't know her that well. Whoever her boyfriend was, I'd think he'd be off the hook."

The front door swung open abruptly, and Wanda snapped, "What are you still doing here? Hank, come inside this instant."

I thought about saying something about my suspicions, but Klein was right. Unless I had more proof, I couldn't just break up the man's marriage. Besides, he'd raised enough doubt in my mind to make me reconsider my stance. Was he telling the truth, or was he just so used to lying convincingly that I couldn't tell the difference?

"Good night," I said, but there was no other response than a repeat of the door slamming in my face.

So who had been lying to me? I wondered as I drove back to River's Edge. Had a thug I was pressuring lied, or had the newspaper editor? On the face of it, Klein was respected in the community, but he wouldn't be the first man in power who lied to save his station in life. One thing Klein had been right about: I needed more proof before I brought the walls of his life tumbling down on him.

When I got back to River's Edge, it was dark. I saw a figure sitting at one of the tables in front of Millie's café as I approached, and I started wishing I'd kept the board I'd used when I realized it was Markum. As the security lights came on, I zipped my jacket and said, "What are you doing out here? It's starting to get cold."

"I'm trying to get used to the temperature for my next job," he said.

"Where are you going, Siberia?" I asked as I sat beside him.

"It's close, but I'm not giving out any more information than that. So what have you been up to tonight? Stumble over any more clues?"

"I'm not sure." After I brought him up-to-date on both of my confrontations, he said, "Harrison, if you're not careful, you're going to get shot one of these days."

"I know I shouldn't have followed him down that dark side street, but I needed to know what he was doing at Becka's."

"Yeah, that was dangerous, too, but I was talking about confronting Wanda Klein. I've heard stories around town about that woman that would curl your toes. Hey, I almost forgot about the run-in you had with her before."

"Don't remind me. I've been trying to come up with the answer since I left Klein's house, but I haven't had any luck. So what do you think? Which man was lying to me tonight?"

"Who had the most to lose?" he asked softly.

"That depends. If the thug thought I might actually club him, he could have. Then again, there's a strong reason to believe that Klein had a good reason to lie."

"Maybe both of them were, then," he said.

"What do you mean? Somebody besides Klein paid those goons to break into Becka's house, but he really was having an affair with her after all?"

"It makes sense, if somebody was trying to get the dirt on the editor. I know he's got a ton of enemies in this town, and it wouldn't surprise me if his own wife paid someone to go after him."

"Great, now I'm more confused than ever," I said.

We sat there in silence a few more minutes, each of us mulling over what I'd discovered, when suddenly there was a voice from the shadows behind us.

Pearly Gray stepped toward us and said, "If I'd known we were having a meeting tonight, I would have worn my warmest coat."

"You're welcome to join us anyway," I said as I pushed one of the chairs toward him with my foot.

"Are you certain I'm not interrupting anything?" he asked.

Markum was quick with his reply. "No, we're just trying to solve the world's problems."

Pearly sat with us. "Wonderful, I just happen to have a solution to most of the planet's woes. The first step would be to emulate the advice of the Bard of Avon."

I grinned. "So what's the second thing we do after we shoot all the lawyers?"

He smiled at me. "Very good, Harrison. Let's see, what should we do after that indeed? After the celebrations are over, at any rate."

Markum said, "We can go after the politicians next, unless anybody has any objections."

When no one spoke, I filled the void. "Motion carried, passed by acclimation. Anybody want to get rid of another group with our third edict?"

Pearly said, "We've turned rather bloodthirsty, haven't we? I should think we've eliminated enough of the undesirables to begin shaping our new world."

"Come on, I'm just getting warmed up," Markum said. "We can do better than that. There are a lot more groups on my list."

Pearly thought about it a moment, then said, "While I'm a peaceable man by nature, perhaps I spoke prematurely."

"That's the spirit," Markum said. "Now who else is going to make our list?"

"How much time do you have?" I asked.

"It sounds as though we're all in the perfect mood for a discussion like this," Pearly said.

By the time we decided to call it a night an hour later, we'd gone through every group, organization and cluster of people who had ever irritated or annoyed us. It would certainly be a quieter world if we were making real decisions, and a much gentler one, too, at least after the initial purge.

After Markum and Pearly left, I went upstairs and found myself out of sorts, pacing around the small apartment wondering what my next step should be. I'd managed to alienate quite a few folks over the course of the day without coming that much closer to the truth. I didn't know how the police ever solved a crime, especially given peoples' tendencies to lie, skew the truth and spin its rationale to always put themselves in the best light possible.

At the rate I was going, all of Micah's Ridge would wash their hands of me before I found out what had really happened to Becka Lane. I didn't care if I left a wake of hurt feelings and crumpled relationships behind me in my questioning. What mattered most was finding the truth, and if parts of my life suffered for it, so be it. It was the least I owed to Becka. For now, all I could do was sleep, so I could start fresh in the morning.

# Sixteen

I'D just opened the candleshop the next morning when an older woman with silver hair and an upright posture came into At Wick's End.

"Hello. May I help you find anything?" I asked.

"I'm looking for Mr. Harrison Black. I understand he's the proprietor here."

"I'm Harrison," I said. "What can I do for you?"

She extended a gloved hand. "I'm Ruth Nash. We spoke on the telephone."

"Mrs. Nash, it's good to meet you. I'd offer you a cup of coffee, but we don't have any here at the shop. We can get some at Millie's, though. It's just twenty feet away."

"Mr. Black, I appreciate the offer, but I'm not here on a social call. I must say, I'm quite alarmed about my brother. I came by to collect you as a courtesy only. Would you care to join me?"

"Absolutely. I'm upset, too. Please, call me Harrison." I figured, what could it hurt to ask her again?

She looked at me with obvious distaste, though I couldn't imagine why. I had on a clean pair of jeans and a new polo shirt.

"If I must," she said. "Now are you coming, or shall I go alone?"

Eve walked in at that moment, ten minutes late. "Harrison, I'm sorry, my car wouldn't start."

"No problem. I need you to watch the store."

She looked at Ruth Nash, then said, "Certainly, it's not a problem."

"Would you like me to drive, or should I ride with you? I should warn you, I've just got two pickup trucks."

"Of course you do," she said. "You may ride with me, if you don't mind."

She started for the door, and I told Eve, "I should be back in an hour."

"What's all this about?" Eve asked me in a hushed voice.

"She's Cyrus's sister. I convinced her to come to Micah's Ridge to talk to him."

"Are you coming, Mr. Black?"

The woman refused to call me Harrison. I decided to let it go.

I was expecting something nice, but not a chauffer-driven limousine. I joined her in back as the heavyset driver held the door for me.

"Thanks," I said. "I didn't realize there was a chauffeur service in Micah's Ridge."

"There isn't. I met the lady at the airport in Charlotte and drove her here."

I couldn't imagine what that bill would look like, but then again, I wasn't paying it.

When Ruth saw I wasn't getting in, she said from the back without showing herself, "Sometime today, Mr. Black."

I tried to squelch my laugh, but the driver had no reaction at all.

As the car started to pull away, Ruth Nash said, "I debated bringing you along, Mr. Black. How can I be certain my brother doesn't have a very good reason not to see you?"

"Ma'am, you go in alone and I'll wait in the car. All I need to know is that he's okay."

She arched one well-sculpted eyebrow. "Mr. Black, enough of this charade. What is the real motivation behind your actions?"

"I told you, this started because of a land deal, but I'm sincerely concerned about your brother. You don't care much for me, do you?"

"And is that important to you, that everyone likes you?"

"Blast it all, I'm not going to let you turn this around against me. I'm the one who called you, remember? I'm worried about your brother, plain and simple. There's nothing sinister about my interest. It's called friendship, whether you choose to believe it or not."

We sat in silence for the rest of the ride to Cyrus's place, which was just fine with me. I hadn't cared for two words the woman had uttered since our meeting. If I wasn't so worried about Cyrus, I would have told the driver to pull over and let me out.

We were nearing Cyrus's place when she finally spoke again. "I may owe you an apology."

"Just one?" I asked.

That finally cracked the icy exterior. "An excellent

point, that. Cyrus and I were raised to be cautious of anyone who claimed to want only friendship from us."

"What a sad childhood that must have been," I said.

She nodded. "While it was true we always had each other, it could be rather lonely at times. If Cyrus has indeed managed to make a friend in you this late in life, I'm pleased."

"Don't be too happy about it. He wouldn't see me, remember? If I've done something to offend him, tell him I'm sorry, would you?"

The car rolled silently to a stop, and I saw that we'd arrived. I started to follow her out of the car when she put a delicately gloved hand on my shoulder. "Mr. Black, would you do me a favor and let me see Cyrus alone?"

"Ma'am, he's your brother. I'm just here as a concerned friend."

"Yes, I'm beginning to believe that. I'll make up the losses due to your absence at the candleshop when I return."

"You see there? You just lost me. I don't want Cyrus's money, and I don't want yours, either."

She said, "Oh dear, I'm not very good at this. I am trying, though."

"Your grandkids must be scared to death of you."

She smiled gently. "Actually they seem to be quite taken with me. I can't say the same for their father, though."

"I don't doubt it," I said.

The driver stepped aside as she started for the door. "Aren't you going with her?" I asked.

"It's not part of my job description," the man said.

"You don't look like the kind of guy who memorizes

the employee handbook. Why not give her a little moral support?"

"If you feel that way, why aren't you going?"

"She doesn't want me," I said, "But she'd probably love to have you."

As the driver and I were talking, Ruth went to the door and rang the bell. I recognized the man who answered, and after a brief but fierce conversation, she turned back toward us. "They turned me away from my own home. I won't stand for it, do you hear me?"

"Yes, ma'am, but I was afraid that might happen. So what do you want to do now?"

"If that cretin thinks he's going to keep me away from my brother, he's sadly mistaken. Mr. Black, would you be so kind as to escort me to the local police department? I believe it's time to go in with force."

"Do you want to talk to a lawyer first?"

She snapped, "I want the Marines, young man, can you understand that? Now direct the driver to the nearest police precinct."

I sat up front and led the driver to Sheriff Morton's office. I stuck out a hand as he drove and said, "By the way, I'm Harrison."

"My name's John," he said as he took it briefly, all the while shepherding the limo through what passed for early morning traffic in Micah's Ridge. "So she's going to sic the cops on them, huh?"

"I think she'd prefer a band of mercenaries, and after talking to her fifteen minutes, I don't doubt she could raise one."

"Should be interesting," he said. When we got to the police department, I held Ruth's door open for her myself.

We found the sheriff wading through a mass of paperwork on his desk. He grunted when he saw me, then came to full attention the second he spotted Ruth.

"Mrs. Nash, I didn't know you were in town."

"I just arrived. That's why I'm here, sheriff. I was rebuffed by some Neanderthal at my own front door. I am still a partial owner of that building. The question is, what are you going to do about it?"

He scratched his head, then said, "Who's keeping you out? Surely it's not Cyrus."

"I haven't seen my brother yet," she said loudly. "That's why we're here."

"And why are you with her?" he asked me.

"I'm a concerned citizen," I said.

"He's here with me, Sheriff. Now round up your men and come with me."

I swear I thought he'd refuse her, or at least try to stall, but the sheriff jumped three feet when she snapped at him.

"I'll follow you in the patrol car," the sheriff said. "You need a ride?" he asked me, obviously wanting to know how I'd managed to get myself so involved in the situation.

Before I could reply, Ruth said, "He's coming with me, sheriff. I mean it, I expect reinforcements."

He nodded. "Yes, ma'am, I'll make it happen."

"See that you do," she said coldly. I was beginning to wonder if there was anyone she liked when she turned to John and said, "Young man, can you find your way back to my ancestral home without Mr. Black's guidance?"

"Yes, ma'am."

"Then do so. Mr. Black, you will ride in back with me."

I climbed in the back of the limo, and we left to visit Cyrus again, this time with our very own cavalry.

I wasn't about to sit quietly by for this round. I followed discretely behind as Ruth returned to front door with the sheriff at her side. As we approached, half a dozen patrol cars pulled in behind us. It would be the perfect time to rob any business in Micah's Ridge, since all the town's police protection was evidently with us.

The sheriff pounded on the front door with his fist. "Open up."

I saw one of the bullies who'd run me off the property earlier swing the door back. "What's with all the racket?"

The sheriff started to push past him, but the man stood his ground. Morton said, "The noise was to get your attention. Now are you going to move, or do my men move you?"

He looked past the sheriff at all of his eager deputies and said, "I don't get paid enough for that. Be my guest."

He stepped aside, and Ruth moved in, Morton half a step behind her and me on their heels. The guard was joined by his fellow employee, and as they started to leave, I said, "Shouldn't you stop them?"

Morton shot me a dirty look, then called out, "Hang around, I'm not finished with you."

"We're just paid employees," one of the men said.

"So who's paying you?"

When neither man would answer, Morton said, "That's what I thought. Magnum, Pruitt, keep an eye on those two."

We walked into the shadows of the house, and Ruth called out for her brother. In a feeble voice we heard him acknowledge our call from the heavily draped living room. "I'm here."

Walking into the dreary space, I saw the ramp I'd noticed from outside.

"Cyrus, must you play these games? Walk out of the shadows to where we can see you."

His voice was softer still as he answered, "That's just it. I can't walk anymore." Cyrus Walters rolled toward us in a wheelchair.

His eyes blazed as he focused on his sister. "Blast it all, Ruthie, what right do you have to be here?"

"Are you saying I need permission to come into my own home, the place I was raised? Nonsense, your thugs weren't about to keep me out. Now what's all this about? Why are you in that chair?"

"I've lost the use of my legs," he said as he buried his head in his hands.

She was beside him in a heartbeat. "Cyrus, is that why you wouldn't see anyone?"

"I was afraid it was getting worse," he said. "I couldn't stand to look you in the eye, Harrison."

Ruth asked, "So it's true then, you two are friends?"

Cyrus nodded. "More than I even realized. He's the only one who wouldn't give up. He got you here, didn't he? Only there's nothing you can do, Big Sister. I can't walk."

"When did this happen?" I asked. "The last time I saw you, you were hale and hearty and striding down your river path."

"It came on me overnight," Cyrus said. "Thankfully the new doctor came to the house to see me. Greg Runion brought him by. He's been giving me injections every day, or else I'd be completely paralyzed by now."

"Do you mean to tell me that you didn't at least consult a specialist? Cyrus, did he rot your brain as well?"

"I couldn't walk, that's all I knew," Cyrus said. "Dr. Jefferson's done something about the pain, but he said my case was hopeless."

"We'll see about that," Ruth said. She told Morton, "Call the hospital. Have them send an ambulance immediately. Then find out the identity of this quack who's been treating him. Do it now, sheriff."

Morton jumped as if he'd been snake bit. "Yes, ma'am, I'm on it."

"I won't go to the hospital," Cyrus said. "They kill people there."

"Well, they cure them there, too, little brother. You've been a perfect fool about this; you know that, don't you? Don't worry though, we'll make it better. Where is that confounded ambulance?"

As if materializing at her request, I heard the sirens approach.

One of the deputies stepped into the room. "Boss, what should we do about those guys you had us watch?"

"Take them in," Morton snapped. "And you can charge them while you're at it."

"With what?" The deputy looked even more confused.

"Make it disturbing the peace, kidnapping, you can even claim they were resisting arrest, for all I care. I just want to sit on them until we can find out who hired them."

"Yes, sir," the deputy said and left.

Two paramedics came in with a gurney between them. "What's happening here?"

Ruth pointed to Cyrus and said, "Take him to the

hospital. He believes something is wrong with his legs, but he's going to resist, I warn you."

"I'm not going to the hospital," Cyrus repeated.

Ruth got down in his face and said, "Little brother, do you really feel like going up against me?"

"No," he said, the fight suddenly gone out of him.

"That's better," Ruth said, softening with capitulation. "Will it help if I ride there with you?"

One of the paramedics said, "Sorry, ma'am, I'm afraid you can't do that."

"Young man, I could stand here and threaten you with the fact that one wing of your hospital was endowed my father, but I won't. Instead, I'll just say that if you do anything to keep me away from my brother, you'll be working in the hospital furnace room before nightfall."

While the paramedic was making up his mind, the other said, "Ma'am, we'd be delighted to have you ride with us."

"Very good," Ruth said, pleased with the minor victory. "Is there any way my brother can avoid being strapped down to that thing and ride upright?"

"I'm sorry, but for his safety, it would be best if we could do it our way."

She nodded. "So be it." Ruth turned to her brother. "I'm going to be right beside you the entire way. Don't worry, Cyrus, I'm here now."

I followed them out, and said, "Should I take the limo and join you at the hospital?"

Ruth said, "No, have the driver take you back to the candleshop. I'll call you later. One second, please," she said as she walked quickly to me. In a low voice, she added, "I'm sorry I doubted you, Mr. Black."

"Then prove it and call me by my given name."

"Harrison it is," she said.

"Ruth? Where are you?" her brother called out.

"I'm coming, Cyrus."

After they were gone, Morton and I stood outside by the limousine. "I guess I owe you an apology," he said reluctantly.

"That's not important right now," I said. "I just hope there's a prayer of a chance he'll walk someday."

Morton nodded. "I owe you one," he said.

I turned to the driver and said, "I need to get back to the candleshop, John. Do you mind giving me a lift?"

"You heard the lady. I'll take you wherever you want to go."

He held the door open for me, but I shook my head. "If it's all the same to you, I'll ride up front."

John smiled softly. "You're one of kind, Harrison. Most folks love being chauffeured around."

I had an idea. "Do you ever get to ride yourself? Give me your cap and I'll let you travel in style. You can even shut the interior window if you want to."

He laughed. "I'd get fired if I did that, but thanks for offering."

Back at the candleshop, I raised a few eyebrows getting out of a limo, but I just waved to Millie as she came out of her shop to see what the fuss was about. John and I shook hands, then he headed off to the hospital.

"Now I've seen it all: Harrison Black riding around town in a limousine."

"I thought it might be fun," I said, keeping my expression level.

"Harrison, you're pulling my leg. Ruth Nash's back in town, isn't she?"

I nodded. "I finally got in to see Cyrus."

"How is he?"

"He was in a wheelchair," I said. "It doesn't look good."

"Then I'll say an extra prayer for him tonight," Millie said.

"It couldn't hurt."

Millie wasn't the only one the limo had attracted. Sanora came out of her shop, too. "Harrison, I need to talk to you."

From the expression on her face, I knew it wasn't going to be a pleasant conversation. "I'll be right there."

She ducked back into her shop, and Millie asked, "What have you done now?"

"I'm not sure, but I've got a feeling I'm about to find out."

# Seventeen

"**H**ARRISON, I hate to be another complication for you, so I've decided to make the decision myself and leave River's Edge."

I stared at Sanora, not sure what the best way to react would be. In a heartbeat, I decided to go with full, flat-out honesty, just as Pearly had suggested. "Blast it all, I don't want you to leave."

She looked at me carefully and asked, "Does that mean Heather is going?"

"How many times am I going to have to say this? Sanora, I want you both here. You're an important part of River's Edge, and I'm not talking about the rent you pay, either. You bring us all a classier level of clientele, and more importantly, I like you being a part of the place."

"Why, Harrison, I didn't realize you cared."

I ran my fingers through my hair. "Listen, I know I've been kind of distracted lately, but I haven't been playing favorites, I swear it. I've been so tied up with everything that's been happening, I haven't had a chance to be the landlord I should be."

She touched my arm lightly. "I know we all make demands on time you don't have."

"I mean it, Sanora, I don't want you to go. It's as simple as that."

She took it in, then nodded firmly. "Then I won't leave. If Heather has a problem with me, she's going to have to just deal with it."

"Good, I'm glad you're staying. I'll run your new lease right over."

She smiled slightly. "Before I can change my mind, is that it?"

"I didn't say that. I want you to be happy here."

She gestured to the river outside. "Why do you think I fought so hard to get back? River's Edge gets in your blood, you know?"

"I do," I said.

I ran upstairs and grabbed Sanora's lease, then almost as an afterthought I grabbed Heather's as well. Maybe I'd be two-for-two today.

Sanora laughed when I barged back into her pottery shop. "You weren't kidding, were you?"

"I even brought you a pen."

She took it, started to sign, then stopped.

"What's wrong?" I asked. "You're not going to change your mind, are you?"

"No, but I hope this isn't an omen or something. The pen you gave me is out of ink."

"Blast it all, I meant to throw that one away."

Sanora grabbed another pen and said, "Don't worry, Harrison, I'm not someone who looks everywhere for hidden signs." She jotted her name down in all the marked boxes, then handed the document back to me. "There, it's official. I'm staying."

"And it's official that I'm glad."

I headed back to my apartment, happy the dry pen had been with Sanora and not Heather. There was no doubt my New Age friend would have indeed taken the dry pen as an omen. I'd have to find a brand-new one before I asked Heather to renew her lease. I took Sanora's signed contract back upstairs, then dug into my desk drawer for a pen that wrote. I found one nearly brand-new and clipped it onto the side of Heather's lease. She was the last one on my list, but from the way things were going, I wasn't at all sure she was going to stay.

The New Age shop she owned had a few folks browsing inside, so Heather wasn't too busy to talk to me.

"I brought your new lease," I said.

"So Sanora's moving?"

"No, she said if you had a problem with her, you were just going to have to deal with it. She's sure you're leaving."

Heather looked at me as if I'd slapped her. "She said that?"

"She didn't have to. She signed her lease. That says it all, doesn't it?"

Heather said, "Give me my lease."

"Wait a second and think about this. As much as I want you here, I don't want to force you to stay."

"If you want me here, give me the lease."

I slid it across the counter, with the pen still attached. She signed her name so hard the lease agreement paper tore under the assault. I said, "Heather, I'm glad you're staying."

She snapped, "Go tell her I'm not budging, either. She's not going to run me out."

I started to leave, but I swear Esmeralda winked at me as I walked past her. I had been reading way too much in that cat's expressions lately. While I wasn't particularly proud of the way I'd manipulated Heather and Sanora into staying, I was happy they were both going to be around. If it turned out that one of them was miserable with the arrangement later, I'd tear up the lease and let them off the hook, and what's more, they both knew it. But I'd given them both a reason to stay, and evidently it had been enough.


"NICE OF YOU to grace the place with your presence," Eve said as I walked into At Wick's End.

"I'm the landlord at River's Edge, too, you know. These new leases have thrown a wrench into everything."

Eve actually looked guilty for chastising me, a first in our working relationship. "I'm sorry, I forgot all about that. Are we losing Heather or Sanora?"

"Guess again," I said, keeping my face expressionless.

"Oh, dear, not both of them. Harrison, you've got to do something."

"There's another option you didn't mention. They're both staying."

Eve startled me by throwing her arms around me in a hug. As soon as she realized what she'd done, she pulled quickly away. "How did you manage it?"

"I had a nudge from Pearly."

There was a history of bad blood between the two of them, so Eve dropped her inquiry. "So the family stays together," she said.

"For now," I amended, fully intending to release anyone from their lease if they ever requested it. River's Edge was more than just a place to do business. Eve was right; it was a family, and if someone wanted to leave, I wouldn't stand in their way.

I was selling a block of bee's wax for pouring when the telephone rang. I'd taken to carrying the portable phone around with me when I worked the candleshop, so it was easy enough to answer as I worked.

"At Wick's End."

"Harrison, this is Jeanie from Greg Runion's office."

"Hi, Jeanie. What can I do for you?"

She said, "Greg's going on a sudden business trip that I didn't know about. I've got a feeling he's not coming back."

"What makes you say that?" I asked.

"He stormed in here ten minutes ago, then rushed out the door again just now with a box full of papers. Harrison, he looked scared, and in all the time I've worked for him, I've never seen Greg Runion afraid of anything. I thought you should know."

"And you don't have any idea where he's going?"

"That's just it," she said. "He always makes such a fuss about traveling. I have to get his tickets, make the hotel reservations, everything. He stopped at my desk and told me he'd be back in a day or two, but I don't believe him. Should you call the sheriff?"

"And tell him what, that your boss decided to leave town? Jeanie, Morton thinks I've got an overactive imagination as it is. There's nothing I can do."

She hesitated, then said, "I just thought you should know."

"I'm sorry, you're right. I shouldn't have been so abrupt. I do appreciate you calling me. Listen, if you come across anything else I should know about, call me back, okay? And thanks again. I mean it."

"You're welcome," she said.

As I finished ringing up my customer's wax, I wondered what had gotten into Runion. Jeanie knew him better than anyone else in the world, and if he was running scared, she'd know it. But what could have shaken him up so much? I wish I knew, but I couldn't do anything about it at the moment.

I waited on another customer or two, happy to be back in the groove of working the candleshop while my mind wandered among the possibilities. Becka's death, Cyrus's mysterious debilitation and Runion's odd behavior swirled through my mind.

I was pulled out of my musings by the chime over the front door. One look at Mrs. Jorgenson's face and I knew I was in serious trouble.

"Harrison Black, I knew you could be dense at times, but I always gave you credit for having a minimum of common sense. It appears that I was wrong."

"Good morning, Mrs. Jorgenson. And how are you today?"

"In your office. Now."

I followed her back to my cubbyhole, wondering what I'd done to infuriate her so much. Eve looked ashen as we walked by, her gaze begging for an answer, too. I just wished I could illuminate things for her. I honestly didn't have a clue what I'd done this time.

We got back to my office and she closed the door

behind us. "What were you possibly thinking? Or was actual cogent thought a part of your process?"

"This might be easier if I knew exactly what you were chewing me out about," I said.

"Have you made any more grievous errors lately that you're blissfully unaware of?"

"Ma'am, it seems lately I've been making them all the time."

"I'm talking about Grover. What did you do, confront him with what I'd told you?"

"I went by to see him. That was your suggestion, wasn't it?"

She fought to control her temper, and after a few moments, she said, "Harrison, it should have been handled delicately. You've done more than jeopardize your chance to eat the best barbeque around here. You've put me in a tenuous position with the man at exactly the wrong time."

"Wait a second," I said. "I never mentioned your name. In fact I made it a point not to."

She picked up a candle-shaped letter opener from my desk. It had been Belle's, and I liked the look and heft to it. What was she going to do with it, though? As angry as she was with me, I was half-afraid she was going to skewer me with it. "Do you honestly believe that in a town as small as Micah's Ridge that it's possible for my visits here to go unnoticed? I daresay everyone in town knows about our candlemaking lessons. Honestly, how hard do you think it was for Grover to decipher where you got your information?"

"I'm sorry, Mrs. Jorgenson, but I honestly didn't mean to hurt you."

She frowned, then said, "Of course you didn't, but

the damage has been done nonetheless. The question is, what do we do about it now?"

"I'll go apologize again, but I doubt it will do any good."

"Harrison, we need to pay him a visit together, and I mean right now."

"You're coming, too?" I asked. It reminded me uneasily of the time as a child I'd taken a candy bar from the store without bothering to pay for it. My mother had marched me back there and lorded over my full confession. I'd learned that lesson well enough, and my criminal act was never repeated.

"Of course I'm coming," she said. "This is too important to leave in your hands."

"Gee thanks. Your confidence in me is overwhelming."

That brought the hint of a smile to her face. "Harrison, you're a wonderful teacher and a skilled candlemaker, but I'm afraid you're out of your league on this one. Let's go."

"Do you honestly mean at this very moment?"

She said, "The sooner we do this, the better. Let your staff handle the store."

"My 'staff' has been covering for me most of the last week."

Mrs. Jorgenson said, "And if she hopes to have a place to work, she'll continue to do so."

I followed her out of the office and called out to Eve. "I'll be back."

She managed to nod, but the worried expression on her face spoke volumes. I wasn't too pleased with the way things were working out, either.

We took her car, and as we approached Grover's

place, I saw that his red T-shirt signal was out on the bush. I said, "This won't work, there will be lots of people around."

"Trust me, Harrison."

I thought it was a bad move, but then my own ideas hadn't been all that hot lately, either. I followed Mrs. Jorgenson as if I were on a leash. There was a smattering of customers sitting at their tables, and I wondered how word managed to spread so quickly that Grover was serving barbeque.

He stared holes through me as I approached. Before Mrs. Jorgenson could say a word, Grover snapped, "He's not welcome here."

"He's with me," Mrs. Jorgenson said.

"You're not bulletproof yourself, you know that don't you?"

She frowned. "Why are you being so difficult about this?"

I felt like grabbing her arm and shaking her. If this was Mrs. Jorgenson's idea of an apology, she could take a lesson or two from me.

"I won't discuss it. Not in front of him."

Mrs. Jorgenson turned to me. "Wait for me by the car."

I nodded, then said to Grover, "I really am sorry."

He didn't acknowledge my apology, though I hadn't expected him to. As I walked back to Mrs. Jorgenson's car, I noticed that not a soul there was willing to make eye contact with me. I suddenly knew how a pariah felt.

Mrs. Jorgenson was back in less than five minutes, and from the expression on her face, she hadn't had any more luck than I had.

"Of all the unmitigated nerve, that man actually banished me from coming back. I still can't believe it."

"I'm sorry I got you into this mess," I said.

"Never mind, Harrison, this isn't about you anymore. If Grover Blake thinks he can treat me like that, he's sadly mistaken. I won't tolerate it."

"But what can you do?"

"More than he realizes," she said tightly, and I was glad I wasn't in Grover's position. I wasn't sure what Mrs. Jorgenson's next move was going to be, but I knew it would most likely be unpleasant for Grover.

She dropped me back at River's Edge with barely a nod, and I went inside At Wick's End, my head hung low. Somehow I'd managed to make things even worse. What else could go wrong?

Unfortunately, I didn't have long to find out.

# Eighteen

**G**ARY Cragg stormed into the candleshop, with Sanora right on his heels. "Harrison, we've got a serious problem."

Sanora added, "They're getting ready to bulldoze the woods beside us."

"What? That can't be."

"Then how else do you explain four bulldozers unloading next door?" Sanora said. "I've seen this before. They won't wait for a permit. They'll go ahead and knock all the trees down, then pay the fines. We've got to stop them!"

"Hang on a second," I said. "I want to call Ruth Nash."

Sanora said, "There's no time for that. We've got to move on this now."

"Give me a chance to do something," I said as I grabbed the telephone. I looked up the number for the hospital, and five minutes later I was talking to Ruth.

"Did you know that they're getting ready to demolish the trees beside River's Edge?" I asked.

"On Walters land? I don't think so."

"I can hear the dozers rumbling from here. Ask Cyrus if he sold that land to Runion, or anybody else for that matter."

"If he did sell it to that scoundrel, he was under some kind of undue influence. They've found drugs in Cyrus's system designed to make him weaker every day. Thank God you called me when you did."

"I'm glad for you, but what do I do about this?"

She barely hesitated, then said, "Stall them for as long as you can. I'll get a lawyer on this immediately."

"I have one standing right here with me, if you'd like to speak with him."

"Is he any good?"

"I'd hate to go up against him," I said simply.

"Put him on."

Cragg had a hurried conversation with Ruth, Sanora growing more and more impatient by the second.

Heather burst into the candle shop. She was so upset, she barely missed a beat when she saw Sanora standing beside me. "Harrison, what's going on?"

"That's what we're trying to find out."

She didn't say anything else, but she didn't leave, either. Cragg whispered again, then hung up. "It's obviously a duplicitous move on Runion's part. There shouldn't be any problem getting an injunction to stop it."

"We don't have time for that, Gary," Sanora said. It was clear why Cragg was so interested in the environment all of a sudden: his crush on Sanora was quite obvious, and what's more, she knew it, and was using it to her advantage.

Heather said, "I've got the chains we used to protest when they razed the old theater downtown."

Sanora looked at Heather and said, "You were a part of that?"

"I want to preserve what we've got, not pave over it," Heather said snippily.

"I wasn't criticizing, I'm impressed," Sanora said.

Heather didn't know how to take that. "Hang on, I'll be right back."

Two minutes later she showed up with a hefty length of chain and a padlock. "I'm going to chain myself to the biggest tree I can find so they can't do anything."

Cragg said, "I don't recommend it. Let me handle this the legal way."

Sanora said, "We don't have time for that. You go do your paperwork and we'll hold them off as long as we can."

"We?" Heather asked abruptly.

Sanora smiled. "You don't think you're going to have all the fun, do you?"

"I thought you were all for development," I said.

"Not like this," Sanora said. "This is where we need to take a stand."

I made up my mind in an instant. "Wait a second. I'm going with you, too."

Eve, who had remained silent through the discussion, piped up. "Harrison, this isn't the kind of publicity we need. You can't afford to offend our customers by being arrested."

"They'll just have to live with it," I said. "I'm doing this for Cyrus, too."

Cragg drove off to the courthouse while Heather,

Sanora and I raced through the woods toward the sound of the bulldozers.

"I hope we're in time," Sanora said.

"We've got to be," Heather answered.

We came into the clearing and stopped behind a giant oak that would be the first tree that had to come down. A crew was unloading the last bulldozer from a massive flatbed truck. Heather said, "We're just in time. Take this end, Harrison."

We circled the tree, putting our bodies inside the loop of steel. Nobody noticed us as we faced the heavy equipment, and once the lock was snapped in place, we stood waiting for someone to see our protest. I tried yelling at the workers to get their attention, but the bulldozers were making too much noise.

The first monster started lumbering toward us, and for a second I didn't think he was going to see us in time to stop. Heather and Sanora joined me as I screamed at him, waving my arms to try to capture the driver's attention. I was silently glad Heather had done this before. What a nightmare it would have been if we hadn't pulled our arms out before attaching the chains.

I could smell the dozer's diesel breath when the operator finally spotted us. He shut off the engine, and a man in a hard hat raced toward him. "Johnson, what do you think you're doing?"

He pointed to us in disgust, and the foreman turned to the other operators and made a killing gesture with his hand at his throat.

The woods were suddenly filled with an echoing silence.

"What do you clowns think you're doing?" he shouted as he stormed toward us.

"We're saving the woods," I said.

"What you're doing is delaying me, and I hate to be delayed. Unlock that chain and get out of the way."

Heather said, "Sorry, we didn't bring the key with us. We're waiting for an injunction to stop you."

"That's not going to happen, lady. You'd better hope you find the key."

"We're not leaving," I said.

"We'll see about that."

He turned to the man on the nearest bulldozer and said, "Run them down."

The operator looked at him like he was insane. "Come on, Mr. Kirk, you know I can't do that."

"Then get out of the seat so I can. They're here illegally, and I'm sick of these tree-huggers trying to stop every job we take on."

The operator climbed out of the seat, and Kirk took his place. "This is your last chance to unlock yourselves and go home like good little boys and girls."

"We can't," I said, a little too loudly in the quiet around us. "She told you, we don't have the key."

"Then I suggest you find it and fast."

He started the dozer up, and I could feel the ground rumble under us as it approached. The blade looked huge as it came closer and closer, and I could see chunks of dried dirt clinging to its steel teeth. At ten feet away, I kept thinking he was bluffing, but by the time he was within five feet of us, I knew we were all going to die. The man had a crazed look in his eyes, as if he'd been waiting his entire career to run somebody over with a bulldozer. He was less than twenty-four inches from us when the dozer stopped and the engine died. I was between Heather and Sanora, and we'd held hands automatically as the bulldozer had approached. They'd each squeezed so hard, I wasn't sure I'd ever get the feeling back in my hands, even if we somehow managed to live through the dozer assault.

Kirk jumped down from the tractor. "You people disgust me." He spat on the ground in front of me, barely missing my shoe.

"Runion doesn't own this land," I said.

"What are you talking about?"

"He doped up the owner so he could trick him into selling. That's a crime, and if you do anything under his orders, you're just as guilty as he is." I didn't know where I stood on legal grounds, but the morality of what I said was real enough.

"I don't know anything about that," he said grudgingly. "All I know is that we're being paid to clear this land and haul off whatever we find."

He turned to one of his men and said, "Bring me the bolt cutters. They're in the back of my truck." Then he said to us, "I've got a job to do, and until Mr. Runion comes and cancels it himself, these trees are coming down. If you won't unlock that thing, I'll do it for you."

"Mr. Kirk? I can't find them," one of his men called out.

"Blast it all to Baal, do I have to do everything myself?" He stormed back to his truck, and I noticed the roughnecks giving him plenty of room, though he was a good fifty pounds lighter than most of them.

I asked Heather, "What do we do now?"

"We resist," she said. "Once he cuts the chain, we all go limp on the ground. We have to make them carry us off."

"So we're beaten," Sanora said.

"There's only so much we can do," Heather said. "They dragged us away from the theater, too, but at least we tried."

I felt both women tighten their grips on my hands again as Kirk approached with a pair of huge red bolt cutters. He was just about to shear the lock when I heard a police siren in the background. I said, "Here comes the cavalry. I wouldn't do that if I were you, you're in enough trouble as it is."

"I didn't lay a finger on you," Kirk said.

Sheriff Morton himself drove up, and Cragg got out of the front seat of the squad car before it even came to a complete stop. The attorney said, "Who's in charge here?"

Kirk looked as though he wanted to deny it, but he finally said, "I am."

"This order states that you must cease and desist all operations until the sale of this land can be properly investigated."

The foreman didn't even look at the document. Kirk turned to his men and said, "Load them up, boys, we're going back to the shop."

There were several groans from his people, but they did as they were told. Kirk himself climbed up onto the bulldozer in front of us, and I didn't breathe again until it was heading safely back to its mates.

"It's okay now, you can unlock the padlock," Morton said.

Heather said, "I lost the key ages ago."

"Then how do we get out of this? Morton, go borrow Kirk's bolt cutters, would you?"

"No need," the sheriff said. "I've got a set of cutters myself. When Cragg came to get me, I grabbed them, just in case." He cut a single link from the chain and we were soon free again. "That was closer than I liked," I said as I stood inside one of the track marks the bulldozer had made. If it did that to the ground, I shuddered to think about what it could have done to us. "Thanks for bailing us out."

Morton nodded to Cragg. "Thank your attorney. I just helped him execute the order."

I saw Sanora go over to Cragg and watched as they had a whispered conversation that ended with her kissing him on the cheek. I swear I thought the attorney was going to faint from the attention.

Heather followed Sanora's example, and though she and the sheriff had had more than their share of clashes in the past, she leaned forward and kissed his cheek as well. He stepped back and said, "I told you, I was just doing my job."

I was feeling left out when both women approached me and planted a kiss on each cheek at the same time. "Thanks for standing up with us," Sanora said.

Heather added, "We knew we could count on you."

They wrapped their arms around me briefly, then the three of us walked back to River's Edge. The woods around us were safe, at least for that day.

Eve was dying to know what had happened when I walked back into the candleshop, but all I said was, "We stopped them."

She was too proud to ask for more details, though the strain of not knowing was obvious on her face. I was about to give in and bring her up-to-date when Pearly walked in.

"I understand I've missed the excitement yet again," he said.

"If you call almost getting run over by a bulldozer while being chained to a tree, yes, I'm sorry you missed it, too. You could have taken my place."

Pearly laughed. "Come now, Harrison. Our country has a long history of civil disobedience. You've just added a paragraph to history."

"If it's all the same to you, I'm perfectly happy being a candlemaker. It's what I was meant to do."

Pearly slapped my shoulder. "One never knows what one can do until called upon in the face of an emergency. I'm proud of you for standing your ground, Harrison."

I was uncomfortable with the praise. "Heather and Sanora should be the ones you congratulate. I never would have done it without them."

"An amazing thing, that," Pearly said. "The two of them are huddled at a table in Millie's café, regaling each other with their past deeds of activism. It appears the women have a common bond undiscovered until today."

"Then at least something good has come of this mess," I said.

"Perhaps for them, but I'm not so sure about you. As I was leaving, I heard them plotting an attack to protest the overdevelopment of Micah's Ridge, and unless I'm mistaken, you'll be playing a key role in the movement yourself."

I laughed. "I'm glad they're getting along, but they're going to have to save the town without me. My protesting days are over."

Eve, who'd dusted the same shelf three times during my talk with Pearly, finally spoke up. "That's the only thing I wanted to hear."

"Don't give me a reason to change my mind," I said, and surprisingly, Eve went back to her dusting.

"Well, I won't keep you," Pearly said. "I just wanted to share in the joy of your achievement."

"I didn't do all that much," I repeated.

"Don't disparage what you've done, my friend. It was a brave act."

"If you say so. To tell the truth, I was scared to death when that bulldozer got close."

"Don't you know that's the true definition of bravery? It's courage in the face of fear, Harrison."

It was good to know I could do something like that if I had to, but I never wanted to be in a position where I felt the need to chain myself to anything ever again.

# Nineteen

**R**UTH Nash came by the candleshop ten minutes before closing time. I hugged her, and despite a bout of initial reluctance, she ended up returning it.

"What was that for?" she asked.

"You saved the day," I said. "They were ready to cut the chain holding us to the tree, and I wasn't sure what was going to happen after that."

"Harrison, I still can't believe you committed such an overt act of civil disobedience."

"To tell you the truth, it kind of surprised me, too. How's Cyrus doing?"

Ruth smiled bravely. "He's much better now. The last of the drugs are fading from his system. I pity Greg Runion; I've never seen my brother so angry. If he were in any condition to get up, I'm afraid he'd go after the man himself."

"Have they had any luck finding Runion yet?"

"No, but the sheriff assures me it's just a matter of

time. Just in case, though, I'm bringing in some friends of my father who know how to handle such things. They are quite skilled at finding people on the run from the law."

"Your dad knew bounty hunters?" I asked.

"He had quite an eclectic collection of friends," she admitted. "I've found it helpful to call upon them from time to time in the past."

I wouldn't wish myself in Runion's shoes for a million dollars, but he deserved whatever he got, and if Ruth's friends could bring him back to stand trial for what he did, so be it.

"I'm just glad Cyrus is better," I said.

"And we have you to thank for that."

"Anybody else would have done the same thing."

Ruth replied, "But you're the only one who did. Harrison, we've been discussing the matter, and Cyrus and I would like to do something to repay you for what you've done."

"Ruth, I appreciate the gesture, but I told you, I had no ulterior motives here, and I don't expect a reward for it."

"Nevertheless, we've decided to deed the land beside River's Edge to the town of Micah's Ridge, so that it will be held in perpetuity by the community. Tomorrow morning, a surveying team and a landscape architect will design new footpaths through the land so everyone can enjoy it. I hope you're pleased."

I said honestly, "I couldn't be happier if you'd given the land to me outright."

"We considered it, but Cyrus warned me of your stubborn streak of pride."

"It's my family's curse," I admitted.

She paused, then asked, "Harrison, isn't there anything we can do to show our appreciation?"

"You could find out why my ex-girlfriend died," I said. "But if that's too much to ask, I'd settle for getting my ban from Grover's barbecue lifted."

"Pardon me?" she asked.

"I was just joking," I said. "You've done enough. Having that woodland beside me undeveloped is all the thanks I need. Will you be heading back to West Virginia soon?"

"As much as my grandchildren miss me, I'll be staying on a few more days until Cyrus is ready to travel. He's coming back with me for a visit to take the opportunity to recuperate."

"Just don't keep him there permanently, that's all I ask."

Ruth smiled gently. "I imagine time with my grandchildren will bring him back to Micah's Ridge soon enough."

After I closed the candleshop, I headed upstairs for a shower and bed. It was amazing how much the earlier rush of adrenaline had taken out of me. I went to sleep, and for the first time since Becka's death, I slept without dreaming. It was a precious gift to be unencumbered by the night terrors I'd been experiencing too often lately.

Ruth returned late the next morning just as I was selling several more packs of sheet wax to the man who'd been in the candleshop buying supplies for his mother. The man raved, "Harrison, you were right. My mother absolutely loves making candles this way! The cookie-cutter shapes are a huge hit with her, and now she's got my kids making them, too. I don't know how we're ever going to burn all those candles."

After he was gone, Ruth said, "I never realized there were candlemaking kits suitable for children. Could you show me something?"

I led her to the section of shelves where our gel candle kits were stocked. After she read the back of one of the kits, she said, "No, that's too messy. What about the selection that gentleman chose for his mother?"

We moved to the aisle where the sheet-wax kits were kept, and I showed her the vast array of cookie cutters we stocked, along with the various colors of honeycombed wax sheets. After giving her a quick lesson, Ruth said, "How delightful. I'll take one of everything."

I had to look at her to see if she was kidding or not. "That's a great deal of supplies," I said. "I hope you aren't doing it as a favor to me."

"Harrison, I'm doing it as a favor to my grandchildren. They love to do anything crafty. Let me jot down the address for you. It will save me a great deal of trouble if you ship the packages there for me."

I looked at Eve, who'd been watching us, and said, "One of each color sheet wax kit, and one of each cookie cutter."

"No, that won't do at all," Ruth said.

"Is it too much?" I asked. "We can scale the order back."

"Actually, it's too little. Each of my three grandchildren need a complete set of everything. I'm afraid I've spoiled them in that way." She studied me a moment, then added, "And no price breaks for me, young man. I expect to pay full retail."

"Actually, I was thinking about charging you extra," I said.

She started to reply when she saw my grin. "Harrison, you mustn't tease me like that. I came out to see if the surveyors have made any progress. In the meantime, allow me to take you to lunch."

"That sounds great. Eve, we'll be back soon."

"So where should we go?" Ruth asked. "My driver can take us anywhere."

"No need, we can walk from here. I'm kind of partial to Millie's place."

Ruth studied the sign. "The Crocked Pot, eh? Well, I'm game if you are."

"You're going to love it," I said as we walked inside. After studying the menu, we ordered, then took a table by one of the windows up front. We could see the Gunpowder River from our vantage point.

"It is quite lovely here," Ruth said. "I'd forgotten that."

"Do you miss it?" I asked.

"I suppose so, but really, wherever my grandchildren are is home to me now."

We ate our lunch, then I walked Ruth to her car. After she was gone, I headed back to At Wick's End, sorry that my new friend would be leaving soon, and taking Cyrus with her. People seemed to drift in and out of my life with an alarming speed. I was just glad Sanora and Heather had found a way to stay.

I walked in the door of the candleshop and nearly stumbled over the threshold when I saw who was waiting for me, the last person on earth I expected to find paying me a visit. It was Grover Blake.

"Grover, how are you?"

He looked me in the eye and said, "I'm not doing well, but I hope to make it better soon."

"Anything I can help with?" I asked.

"You can accept my apology for acting like an old fool, and be my guest for barbecue tomorrow."

I leaned against the counter, trying not to fall down. "Like I said before, I'm the one who's sorry for the way I acted. I don't blame you a bit for banishing me. I shouldn't have pushed you like I did."

Grover looked at his hands, then said, "Let's just say we both have a reason to be sorry for the way we've been behaving and leave it at that." With that he stuck a hand out. "Can we shake on it?"

"Absolutely," I said, taking his hand. He had a black-smith's grip, and I was glad I could return it. "Is it all right if I bring Markum with me?" I asked.

"I've already invited him. You've got yourself a pow-erful ally there, Harrison."

"Mrs. Jorgenson is something, isn't she?" I agreed.

"I was speaking of Ruth."

"You know Ruth Nash?" I'd only mentioned my problem with Grover in passing, and somehow she'd managed to fix the mess I'd made.

"Ruth and I go way back. She's quite a woman."

"She is at that. Maybe we can get her to come, too."

Grover nodded. "I'd be honored to have her at my table."

After he was gone, Eve said, "You certainly manage to collect the oddest assortment of friends, Harrison."

"Eve, that's the nicest thing you've ever said to me."

She looked surprised by my response, but it was true. Sometimes I felt as though my collection of friends was the best thing I had going for me.

Mrs. Jorgenson came by late in the day. I was sur-prised to see her, since we had a class scheduled for the next morning. I said, "Either you're early or I mixed up my days. Isn't our class tomorrow?"

"I've been meaning to talk to you about that, Harrison. I'm here to buy more supplies for myself, but I believe I'm ready to carry on my candlemaking alone now."

"I understand," I said, stunned by the unexpected nature of her declaration.

"Don't look so hangdog, Harrison, I'm not moving on to another craft; I've got candlemaking in my blood. I just want to experiment on my own for a while. You'll be able to live off the order I'm about to place for months."

I looked straight at her and said, "Do you want to know the truth? I'll miss your company a lot more than I'll miss the income from our lessons."

Was that a tear in the corner of her eye? "Harrison, I'll be around, don't you worry about that."

"Then let me grab a cart and I'll help you."

We filled two of them by the time she was finished, and the total was my largest sale to date, a dozen times more than what I'd charged Ruth earlier. For a banner day in sales, it was one filled with sadness, too.

I knew better than to offer her any discounts, but I did manage to slip one of my own candles into her bags as a present. What I'd said was true. I'd become a candlemaker preparing for our lessons, and I'd miss her greatly.

I expected Eve to be despondent when I came back from loading Mrs. Jorgenson's supplies in her car. Instead, she had a wistful look on her face.

"I expected you to be falling apart about now," I said.

"Harrison, we both knew this run would end sooner

or later. Frankly, I'm amazed she stuck with candlemaking as long as she did. From what I've heard in the crafting circles, her time with us was a record."

"I'll miss her more than her money," I said.

"I know you will, but there will be other students and other classes. In the meantime, you should celebrate. You made enough today off two sales to shut the candleshop down for a month and still have money left over."

"You can take some time off if you'd like, but I can't think of anyplace else in the world I'd rather be than right here."

She laughed. "What a difference your time here has made. I had my doubts the first day you walked into River's Edge, I'm not afraid to admit it."

"That made two of us. I've got it in my blood now, though, there's no getting rid of me."

The rest of the day was happily uneventful, and though I still worried about what had happened with Becka, there wasn't much else I could do about it. I sent Eve home early, knocked off five minutes before closing myself, then headed out to the truck to make my deposit for the night.

I was nearly to my truck when someone stepped out of the shadows.

I'd found Greg Runion after all.

Or more accurately, he'd found me, and from the pistol in his hand, it was pretty obvious he wasn't all that happy to see me.

# Twenty

"**WHAT** are you doing here?" I asked him.

"You know what I want. Give me the papers Becka stole from my office and I'll be in my way. Don't worry, I won't kill you if you do what I say."

"What are you talking about, Runion? I don't have any papers."

He glanced back at his SUV and said, "Jeanie couldn't have been lying about that, too. She told me Becka stole the forged contracts for Cyrus's land and gave them to you for safekeeping, along with a packet of incriminating photographs. You had to butt in where you had no business, didn't you? Why did you do it, Harrison? I almost had it all in my hands, and you blew it for me."

"Listen, you've got to believe me. I don't know what you're talking about. Jeanie isn't telling you the truth."

"Now I'm not sure who to believe," he said. "It looks like you're going to have to die anyway, just like that nosy ex-girlfriend of yours."

"So you killed her?"

"Becka didn't want to take the pills, but I forced her to do it. I told her she'd have a better chance beating the overdose than a bullet."

"But why kill her at all? What did she do to you? Is this whole thing about Cyrus and his land?"

Runion snorted. "You really don't know anything, do you? Becka caught me doing something far more criminal than a fraudulent land deal. Before I could rectify a certain situation, she threatened to turn me in. I didn't have any choice."

"The barrels," I said softly. "You were dumping something illegally and she caught you at it." The pieces all began to fall into place. "You stashed them on Cyrus's land, didn't you? They're somewhere near here. That's why you had to go after him, so you could get control of his land."

"Amazing, you got it on the first try. Too bad it's not going to do you any good. As soon as I take care of you, I'm going to finish Jeanie off, too." Runion glanced back at his SUV, and I didn't doubt she was back there. He continued, "She deserves it if anybody does; she's nearly as guilty as I am in all this. Maybe a lover's suicide pact between you two will work for the police. They bought Becka's death without much problem." He smiled, but there wasn't the slightest bit of warmth as he added, "I'm really going to enjoy killing Jeanie. I can't believe how many times she's lied to me in the last hour. You know, my life would have been so much easier if everyone had cooperated with me to begin with."

His finger tightened on the trigger, so I said, "You're right. I was lying. I've got the packet. I just didn't know what was in it. I'll get you what you came for, but you have to let Jeanie go if I do."

"So she can run to the police and lie to them, too? I don't think so."

"Runion, I'm offering you a head start. If you kill us both, the police will find what you're looking for before you will."

"I didn't think you had the papers," he said.

"Hey, a man's entitled to bluff, isn't he?" I was hoping he'd buy it, since it was something Runion would have done himself. If I fed him enough of a premise of trickery and double-crossing, it might just save my life, and Jeanie's, too.

The gun lowered somewhat, and his finger eased. "So where are they?"

"Not just yet. She goes free first."

"Why do you keep trying to save Jeanie? She's far from innocent here."

"I don't believe you."

"Harrison, there's no way I'm going to let her go."

"Okay," I said, thinking fast. "Then bring her upstairs with us. Once you see what I've got, we'll make the trade."

He thought he had me, I could see it by the way his pupils dilated. I was going to have to do something when we got to my apartment, but at least I'd bought some time.

"Yeah, I guess that will work. Let me get her." He jabbed the gun in my direction. "If you run, she's dead."

"I'm not going anywhere," I said, and I meant it. There was no way I wanted Jeanie's blood on my hands.

She was gagged and her hands were tied when he pulled her out of the SUV.

"Untie her, Runion."

"No way, and I'm not taking the tape off her mouth, either. She can walk fine just the way she is." He told Jeanie, "Don't get any bright ideas. Harrison and I had a long talk while you were in the car. He knows you're just as guilty as I am."

As the three of us started for the front of the building, I said, "So you were the one who sent the goons to Becka's apartment after she died?"

"Yeah, I knew she had a picture there, or some kind of evidence, but they didn't find it."

"That's because I got there first."

That caught his attention. "Good, I can get it when we're upstairs, too."

"Sorry, Markum's keeping it in a safe place."

"I knew you two were in on this together," he snapped. "I'll deal with him later."

"There's going to be a rash of suicides not even Morton's going to buy," I said as he pushed Jeanie forward.

"Don't worry. Markum's going to have an accident, and a bloody one at that."

Oh, great. Now I'd gotten my best friend into the same jam I was in. I kept hoping for inspiration as we climbed the stairs, but none came. Maybe Markum had seen what had happened and was waiting on us on the second-floor landing.

The hallway was empty.

It looked like our time had finally run out.

Once we were all inside, Runion seemed to relax. "So where's the stuff?"

I had a sudden thought and decided there was nothing to lose by going for it. "The papers are in a storage bin on the roof."

"Come on, Harrison, you've got to be kidding."

"It's the safest place I know. The only access is through my bedroom closet."

"Then lead the way."

"I'll grab your papers and come back down," I said as I showed him the scuttle.

"I don't think so. For all I know you have a telephone up there. I'm coming with you."

"Come on, what am I going to do? Jeanie can't climb up, not with her hands tied."

I was hoping that if he untied her, we might have a better chance against him than we did at the moment. I didn't know if she was as guilty as Runion claimed, but Jeanie was the only one I had on my side who might be able to help me out of this jam.

Runion considered it a few seconds, then said, "No, I can't watch both of you when you're up there." Runion grabbed Jeanie as she shot me a look of disbelief. "It's okay," I told her.

"Yeah, keep telling yourself that," Runion said. "Just stand right there, and don't try anything stupid." He led her to the bathroom, shoved her roughly inside, then I watched helplessly as he duct-taped her to the towel bar. Too bad the builder had imbedded it in concrete. The bathroom was industrial, and I doubted she'd ever be able to pull herself free. To be on the safe side, Runion took a chair and jammed it under the doorknob once he locked her in, yanking on it to see if it would hold.

I was going to have get out of this without Jeanie's help.

Runion nudged me with the gun and said, "Let's go, I don't have all night."

I started climbing the scuttle steps, unbolted the

hatch, then threw it open. I figured I'd have five seconds before Runion could join me up there, but as I scrambled for something, some kind of weapon to use against him, he popped his head up, the revolver pointed right at my gut.

"Stand over there," he commanded. "Don't you have any lights up here?"

"I never come up at night," I lied. I was hoping he'd missed the flashlight I kept inside.

He did. At least that was something. Once Runion joined me up there, he said, "So where are they? I hate being up high."

I started going for the storage box, thinking I might be able to use the umbrella to knock the gun out of his hand, but then I thought better of it. If I was going to die, it wasn't going to be defending myself with an umbrella.

Maybe I could use his fear of heights to my advantage. I veered away from the storage bin and walked toward the edge of the roof without slowing down. Thankfully there was a new moon, giving barely enough light to see the sky with. The roof was dark and I was having trouble seeing the edge, but I knew if we stayed up there much longer, both of us would start to get our night vision and my newly formed plan wouldn't work.

"Hey, that's far enough," he said.

"Why don't you wait right here and I'll grab the papers, if you're scared."

Runion made a short bark of a laugh. "I'm not afraid of anything, candle man."

I got as close to the edge as I could, trying to see some discernable line where the building ended and the air started. There, I caught a glimpse of it at the last second. It was time to act. If I got shot, at least I would die trying to save myself.

Runion was too close behind to stop as I whirled, grabbed his gun arm and swung him around. Two shots went off, and I felt one of them whisper past my cheek. I let him go, more out of reaction than plan, and Runion's foot missed the edge. He fell thirty feet screaming, and the noise stopped only after he hit the ground.

I didn't know if he was alive or dead, and at the moment, I didn't care.

I hurried down the scuttle steps, thought about freeing Jeanie, but decided to check on Runion first. Not without reinforcements, though. I banged on Markum's door, and to my relief, he answered.

"I'm on the phone," he snapped, until he saw my face. He said, "I'll have to call you back." After he hung up, Markum said, "What happened? Were those gunshots I heard? Are you bleeding?"

"Come on. I need your help. Bring your phone, too."

I was in no mood to explain myself, and Markum accepted it. We hurried down the stairs, and I worried that Runion would be gone, like a scene from a bad teen scream movie. He was still there, though, the pistol he'd held on me lying ten feet away from him. At first I thought he was dead. Then I heard him moaning, and I knew the fall hadn't killed him. I didn't know whether I was happy about that or not, since he'd killed Becka and had been prepared to kill Jeanie and me as well. Ultimately I knew I'd be happy that I hadn't killed him with that shove off the roof, but for the moment the urge to pick up that pistol and use it was nearly overwhelming. Markum waited, watching me, and as soon as the moment passed, he said, "You made the right decision. Let the courts chew this guy up."

I nodded, amazed that I could have felt the desire to kill him, even if it had passed as quickly as it had come.

"Do you want me to call the cops first, or an ambulance?" Markum asked.

"He's not going anywhere. Call nine-one-one and let them decide."

I started back to the front of the building, and Markum called out, "Where are you going? Morton's going to want to talk to you."

"He can wait," I said. "There's somebody upstairs who needs me."

"He didn't shoot somebody else, did he?"

"No, but he was going to. I'll be right back."

I went upstairs and freed Jeanie. Pulling the tape off her mouth had to hurt, but if she felt it, she didn't let on. "Where is he?" she said angrily.

"He's down on the ground. I pushed him off the roof."

"I hope you killed him," Jeanie said.

"Sorry to disappoint you, but he's still alive."

She pushed past me, and I asked, "Where are you going?"

"To finish the job," she said.

I put a hand on her shoulder. "I understand the impulse, but I already called the police."

"Maybe I can get to him before they can." I couldn't believe sweet Jeanie was ready to finish what I'd started with Runion. I was more afraid of her at the moment than I had been of her boss.

I followed Jeanie downstairs. She stopped abruptly at the door when she saw two police cruisers pull up with their red lights flashing. She turned to me. "Don't say anything about what you've heard. If Runion manages to pull through, we'll claim he's lying."

"I don't fully understand what's going on here."

"There's no time to explain it all now," she said. "Just go along with me on this and I'll make you rich."

I grabbed her shoulder and spun her toward me. "Make the time. What's going on, Jeanie?"

"I've got enough evidence from Becka to hang Runion, but I don't want to use it unless I have to. Your old girlfriend trusted me, can you believe that? I wasn't sure if Becka told you anything, so I started hanging around here. I knew Runion was getting ready to run. I finally found his account numbers for the Bahamian bank, and I've been looking for a way to get his money for years. Why do you think I stuck with him all that time? It surely wasn't because of his personality. Harrison, he's got two million dollars squirreled away somewhere. I've got everything we need to claim it in my pocket. It means that a half a million is yours just for keeping your mouth shut."

"Where'd the money come from?" I asked.

"Runion scammed most of it from Cyrus and Grover. Come on, Harrison, they're both so rich, they won't even notice it's gone. That's a lot of money I'm offering you to stay quiet about it."

"I don't think so," I said.

She studied me for a second, then said, "You're tougher than I thought you were. Okay, we'll split it down the middle, even if you are blackmailing me. I'm being more than fair here, Harrison, considering I did all the work. I helped cheat them both; even Runion admitted he couldn't have done it without me. Are you ready to go?"

"I am now," I said.

We walked outside to where Runion had fallen, and I saw the paramedics working on him. "How is he?" I asked.

"He's got two broken legs and a broken arm. He's going to make it, but he's going to be in a world of hurt in the meantime."

"I can live with that," I said.

Morton said, "What happened here tonight, Harrison?"

"Runion thought I had something that belonged to him, but I didn't." I saw Jeanie watching me closely. I added, "Markum, do you still have that torn picture we got from Becka's place?"

"It's up in my office. Why did he want that?"

"Becka found out Runion was dumping barrels of chemicals on Cyrus's land, and she was trying to turn him in. He got wind of it, so he killed her." I stared at Morton. "He admitted it to me, sheriff."

Morton shook his head as the ambulance sped off. "Harrison, I'm sorry. What can I say? I dropped the ball on this one. Is that all you have for me? I've got his weapon, and Markum told me Runion took a couple of shots at you up on the roof. If nothing else, we can get him for attempted murder and assault for what he did to you and Cyrus. Harrison, you should get that cheek looked at."

"It barely scratched me," I said as I watched Jeanie's expression. She looked absolutely ecstatic that I hadn't said anything about the money to the sheriff.

Morton was just about to his cruiser when I called out, "One more thing you should know."

"What's that?"

I pointed at Jeanie. "He kidnapped her, too, but she's

not entirely innocent here. If you search her, you'll find the number for a secret bank account worth two million dollars, jammed with money that rightfully belongs to Grover and Cyrus. She was getting ready to steal it for herself when Runion caught her."

"You fool," Jeanie said as she launched herself at me. She never made it. Markum grabbed her shoulders and restrained her, then Morton took over from there. "You could have been rich, you idiot," she snarled.

"It wouldn't have been worth it if I had to keep looking over my shoulder for you every second of the rest of my life," I said. "Thanks, but no thanks."

Morton shoved her in the back of the patrol car. "What say you come downtown with me and we'll talk about this?"

"I didn't do anything," she screamed.

"Not from a lack of trying," the sheriff said.

After they were gone, Markum said, "You've had a busy night, haven't you? It's not every man who could turn down a million dollars like that."

"You would have, though, wouldn't you?"

Markum thought about it a moment, then said, "Let's just say I'm glad I wasn't the one she offered it to."

# Twenty-One

RUTH Nash came by the candleshop the next day. "I understand you had some excitement out here last night."

"Too much for me," I said, touching the bandage on my cheek. I didn't want to think about what might have happened if that bullet had hit me a few inches over. As it was, I'd endured a tetanus shot at the hospital, but it hadn't required stitches. "Have they told you what Runion was doing on your brother's land?"

"I've been on the telephone with the Environmental Protection Agency all morning. I finally found someone with enough authority to look into it, and they now reluctantly admit they received Becka's information and were getting ready to act on it."

"Do you believe them?" I asked her.

"I do, since my favorite congressman happens to be on the Ways and Means committee. They'll have a team here by nightfall, and clean-up should begin by morning.

Harrison, you'll have your park before you know it, I promise you that. It's the least I can do, given all you've done for us."

Ruth startled me by offering a hug. I stepped into her arms, held her for a full minute and then she released me. She said, "If you're ever in West Virginia, I hope you visit us. It's beautiful country up there, too, you know."

"If I can ever take a few days off, I might just take you up on that."

"You're always welcome in my home, Harrison. Cyrus is waiting out in the limousine. He'd like a moment of your time, if you can spare it."

"You know it," I said, and I followed her outside. Cyrus looked good sitting in the back of the car, though he had a blanket wrapped around his waist. I gave him my hand, and he did his best to give a firm shake in return.

"I don't know what to say," Cyrus said.

"Just say you're coming back someday," I said. "That's all I need."

"Thank you," he said simply.

"You're welcome," I replied. We locked gazes, then he said, "Ruth, are you quite ready? If we're driving, let's do it now."

John shut Cyrus's door and walked around the car to open Ruth's. She said, "He's getting fussy, so that's how I know he's finally on the mend."

"What did the doctors say?"

She scowled. "The drugs he was given are out of his system, but it's going to take some time for him to recover fully. By the way, the sheriff stopped by the house this morning. They found the charlatan who drugged him. It sounds as though he's going to jail for a very long time. Sheriff Morton also asked me to tell you that Runion and Jeanie are turning on each other. Evidently she played a more active role in this than anyone realized, so we have you to thank for her incarceration as well. I was gratified to hear that you turned her bribe down, but Cyrus said he would have been shocked if you'd done otherwise." She leaned forward, kissed my uninjured cheek gently, then got into the car.

I waved good-bye, but instead of going back to the candleshop, I decided it was high time I went back out onto the water by myself. It felt good the second my kayak hit the Gunpowder, and as I coasted by what would soon be a park, I saw a team of men in white suits working to remove the last of the barrels Runion had dumped there.

Becka would be pleased, I knew, but there was one more thing I could do to honor her memory. Since she didn't have any living relatives, there was no one to give the thousand dollars to that Markum and I had found in her apartment.

I decided to buy the nicest bench I could find, place it along the path, and have a plaque installed that would say:

"There is not enough darkness in all the world to
put out the light of even one small candle."
—*Robert Alden*

I knew in my heart that Becka would have appreciated that.

# Dorothea Hurley's
# Orange Slice Muffins

*This is another recipe from my late mother-in-law,
a blessed woman who believed that no meal was complete without
a slice of pie or a baked treat, and that included breakfast.*

*¾ cup margarine or butter*
*2 cups sugar*
*3 eggs*
*3½ cups flour*
*2 teaspoons baking soda*
*4 teaspoons cinnamon*
*1 teaspoon nutmeg*
*½ teaspoon cloves*
*½ teaspoon salt*
*3 cups applesauce*
*1 box raisins (16 oz.)*
*1 bag orange slice candies (16 oz.)*
*(Optional 1 cup chopped nuts)*

Cream the margarine or butter and sugar, then add eggs
and beat. Alternately, add the sifted mixture of flour,
baking soda, cinnamon, nutmeg, cloves and salt; add
the applesauce to the mixture. Add raisins and orange
slice candies (nuts, too, if you want them), and place the
mixture in greased muffin or loaf pans.

The dough will make two large loaves or 30 muffins.
Bake at 325 degrees for 90 minutes (loaf ) or 20 to 25

minutes (muffins), testing with a toothpick in the center—when it comes out clean, it's ready.

These are great hot out of the oven or frozen, then defrosted in the microwave as needed. We especially like this recipe during the holidays.

# Candlemaking Tips: Poured Candles

Once you've mastered the basic pouring techniques, it's great fun to use different, creative mold forms you can scavenge on your own. For example, egg shells make fascinating candles on their own. Any shape that can handle the hot wax can be converted into a candle. A teapot makes a particularly nice candle as well.

Chunk candles of preset wax can make a beautiful candle. For a more ethereal look, trying adding ice to the mold just before the pour.

If your candle sticks to the mold, try putting it in the refrigerator to cool it.

If your candle looks frosty or has white horizontal lines, the wax was probably too cool when you poured.

If there are tiny pinpricks all over the candle, the wax was probably too hot when you poured.

If there are cracks in your candle, it probably cooled too quickly.

Bubbles in the base of the candle could mean the water bath level wasn't high enough.

Have fun, and don't be afraid to experiment with dyes and scents as well as unique shapes.

The Candlemaking mystery series by

# Tim Myers
*Each book includes candlemaking tips!*

## Death Waxed Over
0-425-20637-8

On Founder's Day, Harrison Black, owner of
At Wick's End, has a stand near Gretel Barnett. When
she's killed in the middle of the festivities—and folks
start suspecting Harrison—he must figure out who
extinguished his biggest rival.

## Snuffed Out
0-425-19980-0

When the power goes out in Harrison Black's candle
shop, he find his tenant electrocuted. Now, as the
tenant's death starts to look like murder,  Harrison will
burn the candle at both ends to catch a killer.

## At Wick's End
0-425-19460-4

Harrison Black has to learn the art of candlemaking
fast when he inherits his Great-Aunt Belle's shop,
At Wick's End. But when someone breaks into the
apartment Belle left him, Harrison begins to suspect
that her death may not have been an accident.

**Available wherever books are sold or at
penguin.com**

The Lighthouse Inn mystery series
by

# TIM MYERS

## Innkeeping with Murder
0-425-18002-6
When a visitor is found dead at the top of the
lighthouse, Alex must solve the mystery and capture
the culprit before the next guest checks out.

## Reservations for Murder
0-425-18525-7
Innkeeper Alex Winston discovers a new attraction
at the county fair—a corpse.

## Murder Checks Inn
0-425-18858-2
The inn is hosting guests gathered to hear the
reading of a scandalous will. But the reading
comes to a dead stop when Alex Winston's
uncle is murdered.

## Room for Murder
0-425-19310-1
Alex's two friends are finally tying the knot. Now
Alex has some loose ends to tie up when the
bride-to-be's ex turns up dead on the inn's property.

B178